Silent Links

– M. S. THORNBER –

www.fast-print.net/store.php

Silent Links
Copyright © M. S. Thornber 2014

A catalogue record for this book is available from the British Library

ISBN 978-178456-086-7

An environmentally friendly book printed and bound in England by
www.printondemand-worldwide.com

This book is made entirely of chain-of-custody materials

Margaret Thornber has lived all her life in the East Midlands and was educated at a Nottingham Convent School, and afterwards completed her qualifications for teaching in Nottingham.

She is married with two sons and six grand children. Her extensive global travels now include Australia where half of her family currently live.

Margaret's experience in writing covers a broad spectrum. After winning a poetry competition at senior school, she widened her skills writing and producing plays for children during her teaching career. She now includes travel writing, poetry and short stories in her portfolio. She was the outright winner of a short story competition and the anthology was published in 2013.

To my husband Max who has always been ready to listen, support and become my mentor.

To Bruce & Sue

True Jriends who showed
patience & encouragement
during the writing process.

Thank you
Margaret.

M.S. Thomber

Characters in Silent Links

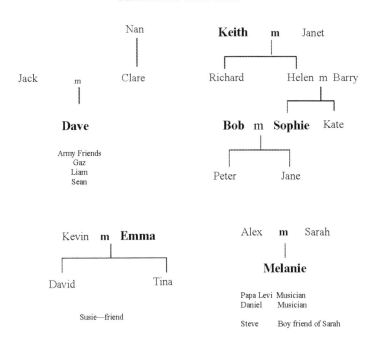

Nan

Keith   m   Janet

Jack   m   Clare   Richard   Helen m Barry

Dave   **Bob**   m   **Sophie**   Kate

Army Friends
Gaz
Liam
Sean

Peter   Jane

Kevin   m   **Emma**   Alex   m   Sarah

David   Tina   **Melanie**

Susie—friend

Papa Levi   Musician
Daniel   Musician

Steve   Boy friend of Sarah

Romeo & Juliet

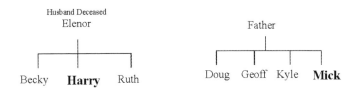

Husband Deceased
Elenor   Father

Becky   **Harry**   Ruth   Doug   Geoff   Kyle   **Mick**

Prologue

T he local council methodically and unobtrusively was working to improve the neighbourhood. Consultations over the use of land had been published and none of the residents had accessed their rights to oppose them. The apathy of ordinary householders could be explained with the priorities of everyday life. There would be the usual protests after the event, but the council was sure they could justify its actions and remind them of the nearby recreation centre set up last year.

Retail outlets were to replace the park area, giving much needed jobs for the young and old alike.

The tree was in the way. It had to go. It was old anyway, probably diseased. The history of the decades it had seen and existed alongside didn't enter into the bureaucracy of progress. The tree couldn't speak of these things, progress must continue.

The councillors congratulated themselves that a decision had been reached, passed and tomorrow would be implemented. A tree removal team was set up for nine o clock and their plans would go ahead.

One more day left for the tree to give its shade and succour. One more day to witness the rainbow of people who would utilize its existence.

M. S. Thornber

Chapter 1

6.00 a.m.

The small piece of shrapnel, like a knife, pierced and stung in Dave's shoulder as he stretched awkwardly on the hard bench. The warm humid air had been too much last night, and his sleeping bag lay on the bare earth, resembling a cocoon. The shrapnel, too small to be operated upon, moved randomly and reminded him sporadically of his past chaotic years with the army in Iraq.

His greasy hair, once blond and thick, stuck to his head with sweat. It hung like a veil over his blue listless eyes. Dave had always been well built and his natural athleticism had been honed into hard muscle and stamina during his army years. Now a shadow of the man he used to be, muscles had wasted with neglect and Dave was difficult to recognise as a young man of twenty seven.

Dismissing the pain and disturbing thoughts, he could hear the early morning noises of the dog walking fraternity resound across the park. The bench was ideally situated under a massive Sycamore tree, old and gnarled. Over the years the farms and hamlets had given way to a modern urban sprawl. Now only the tree remained in the landscape from those forgotten years, placed in this green oasis in an urban desert.

The nearby church bells chimed six times as he hastily gathered his few belongings, anxious to be away before any gardeners or park officials appeared. They had little sympathy for the homeless.

He cast his mind back to why he had ever joined the army which had ultimately been his downfall. Sixteen years old, as an eager youth, he had signed on giving his life over to them. Dredging into his mind he asked himself why he had ever made that decision. His disjointed thoughts led him through the chain of events.

The fatal accident had torn his life apart. With both his parents suddenly dead, Nan had been his only relation left when he woke up that fateful morning. He remembered the hurt of the past and his mum's words.

"Why don't you want to come with us?" she had questioned that morning. How could he have explained? He was only thirteen, his mind and body struggling with hormones and feelings. He had never had to share his dad with rival brothers and sisters. No, he competed with his dad's all consuming main interest, athletics.

"Running, running, running, that's all I've done in my life!" grumbled Dave under his breath. He relived the pain he felt after training hard even though his young body was used to the sessions. That predestined morning, he had longed to stay in bed relaxing.

"Dad and Mum can manage without me in the team just this once!" he argued inwardly. The trio regularly accompanied the athletic team at competitions.

Dave never bothered much about these track events that relentlessly followed week after week. His dad's passion and dedication to his son winning, proving he was the best, seemed pointless to him. He loved pushing his young body to improve, it gave him freedom within himself, and that was satisfaction enough. He knew his mother felt this too, as often they would run together on the track, lap after lap in harmony. No words were needed, they held this secret buzz between them.

The youngsters enjoyed the banter that spread amongst the team. They were mates struggling to exceed their own limitations and congratulating each other as they reached their goals. Dave couldn't picture them as adversaries or competitors to himself. He could see his father's mystified expression that he wasn't compelled to be first. He was usually unaware when he was in front of the pack, just intent on pounding the track in his own world.

Dave knew he disappointed his father and he often wondered what his dad would say if he gave up running. Would he love him just as much? Instinctively he realised that he would see and have less time with his parents. Other rivals who were hungry for results would eat up more and more of family time. Would his dad even be interested in him? What part could he play in family conversations?

His mum Clare had colluded with him that day, recognising that pushing their son might back fire on his future. She had disguised his reluctance to join them, feigning his sickness, the real reason wasn't spoken by either of them. Nan would step in, spoil and cosset him just this once.

"It was my fault, I should have been there with them," Dave muttered to himself recalling the past and living it once again.

The news of the crash had hit the thirteen year old like a hammer, but it was several weeks before he felt what he had lost. The special bond between father and son had been strong, Dave was showing signs of a future star on the track. Clare knew how proud Jack was of his son, it haunted her that Dave was their only child, Jack would have loved more, he had so much patience and enthusiasm.

They had met on the track and were both talented athletes, Jack blond and muscular, Clare the opposite, dark, slight and agile. Their whole life revolved around sport. Marriage and their first child were absorbed into the mix. Jack doted on his son, and Dave, a carbon copy of his dad followed and imitated him. The tiny baby quickly grew into a demanding toddler who seemed to run before he took his first staggering steps. Jack's pride grew as his boy so obviously loving to run on the track, developed naturally into the sport. As he excelled it was hard to calculate if father or son was the motivating force. Certainly Jack relived his focus for athletics through his boy and basked in the successes that came with it. A goal or pinnacle for Dave hung there unspecified but it was the driving force for his dad's actions and pep talks!

The blame Dave felt for refusing to go swamped him during those first days after the car crash. Zombie like he trailed around after Nan, making cups of tea and organising the funeral. Nan, although a rock in the daytime, gave way to a heaving weeping huddle that Dave could hear through the door to her bedroom. He tried to comfort her but knew that they were miserable attempts. She had lost her only child.

There were few family members attending the funeral but the church was filled with Jack and Clare's friends from the sporting life they had led. Dave knew in his child's heart they were not there for him. Sharing his parents with them and the sport had led to this place, he wouldn't turn to these other people, ever.

Nan and he struggled on in the next weeks, reorganising their lives and slowly emerging from the blackness. Routines and structure helped, but the heart of their life had evaporated. In the swirling vacuum they held on to each other but the needs of a teenager and pensioner were so disparate.

As Dave grew sensitive to his Nan's needs, he felt the security she gave him and isolated himself further from any other influences. He hung on fiercely to the image of his dad's strong jaw line and mother's laughing eyes. Dave became a master at avoiding school, 'bunking' off with his mates and evading Nan's questions. He built a web of confusion around his daily life prevaricating at any demands and keeping teachers and Nan apart.

He had exploited her weariness as she struggled to contain his unmanageable behaviour. She fed and clothed him but didn't have the skills to motivate him, only love him and trust in the future. Dave, however, thought that school was a necessary evil and thoughts for a career or prospects were pushed away in favour of short term satisfactions.

'What do we need maths or science for?' he could hear Bob, his friend's voice echo in his ears.

"Let's skip out after registration," Joe would say, " we can try out the skate boards at that new place."

There were few occasions that a lone voice could change their minds.

"McDonalds has a great offer on, we can get back for rugby without old Ellis finding out," another would contribute. Dave's circle of mates, predictably, were of one mind, that school held nothing for them. Gathering together, whenever they could abscond, they met in McDonalds, laughing, enjoying the fruitless days until they could leave.

Sophie, subtly insinuating herself into the scene had halted the downward spiral for him. Small and dainty, he hadn't noticed her at first, until her bright hazel eyes had focused on him. She stood out from the crowd, she wasn't loud or brash. She didn't have any quick or smart answers to reduce those around her. He watched and waited, drawn towards her. Surprisingly, she was responsive and they became a pair. Her influence upon him began to take root. He began to reconsider that there might be some point to education as he followed in her wake.

"I don't want to waste my life," Sophie would say, "I want to be a nurse, maybe a doctor, it's something I've always wanted to do though I don't know if I'll be good enough."

"Course you will," Dave urged her. He couldn't see how anyone as brainy as Sophie would have any problems.

"You can't rely on anything for certain Dave," she would respond, "I need to work for my dreams, they won't just happen."

"It doesn't matter for me, there's no one to prove anything to," he persisted.

Sophie's irritation would spill over and she would argue that now was the time and place to use his brain and to follow his own dream. Dave felt so lucky that she was bothering about him, and caring about his future. She was diligent but fun, allowing him to argue his ideas, without making him feel stupid. He loved her intensely. She was his first love and, with her in it, the world became a brighter place.

Discovering that Bob had muscled in and taken Sophie out, was a betrayal by two people he thought he could trust. Sophie, Bob, surely they were his friends? How could they deceive him in this way? Was she about to leave him, just like the others in his life? In an emotional cauldron of thoughts and feelings, he inevitably reverted to old habits. It seemed no one could reach him to reason or help.

Before the term ended, Dave had nagged Nan into giving her permission to enlist in the army, spurning advice from those around him. It reminded Nan of her husband's passion for an army career. Confused and upset at the speed of events she waved him off with anxious thoughts hidden deep inside her. She returned to salvage what little life she had left, without the last of her family.

Army, while a love or hate environment for many, was both for Dave. Resisting initially the strict regime of every day, slowly he began to relax and feel the framework around him. A structure that held and comforted him in a peculiar way. Small irritations became a lifeline in this reliable and predictable background.

He began to find pleasure as part of a huge machine, a cog in a complicated wheel. The chain of command strong and loud, he jumped at orders barked at him without resistance. The parading, drilling, endless cleaning duties and other physical challenges were tackled with more enthusiasm than Dave had ever shown. Increasingly he felt himself eager to do something well, to be the best. The new recruits around him were forging into a group, helping and encouraging each other.

Basic army training was a team building situation, where each individual became a vital part of the whole unit. Relying and depending on every person was essential, something Dave had learned to do without. In his grief he had even rejected these benefits as unrealistic.

So Dave thrived, along side three mates who became inseparable. Gaz, Liam, Sean and he bonded in such a way that they could know each others thoughts in most situations. The basic training well over, they settled into their home barracks and waited for their first posting.

Drinking binges and sprees around town became part of their free time but never detracted from their reliability to the army. They were ready and eager to put themselves to the test on any engagement with the enemy. Caution and sense from older comrades could not deter their eagerness or puncture their naivety. At last the posting to Iraq was known and all preliminaries at home were completed, they were deployed and on their way, content to settle back to the droning of the plane.

The heat, smells and noise in this foreign land assaulted their senses as they stepped onto the tarmac. Similarities in the army routine back home changed into new orders to survive and thrive in this hostile place. They quickly learned to rely on each other, it was more than essential, it was vital! They became rocks to each other. No one could have prepared them for how vulnerable they felt. An outward appearance of confidence and surety masked their inner turmoil and nightmares. Each day they pushed it away, went about their duties and reassured each other.

The poverty of the people overwhelmed Dave initially, particularly where the fiercest action had taken place. Shelled and broken buildings were once the homes of these people. The little they had blasted away, children scrabbled in the dust to salvage small treasures. The heat and dust a constant enemy to combat. The unit struggled to adjust their bodies to soaring temperatures and freezing nights.

Dave had rarely dealt with blood or injuries before but now the reality of human frailty hit home. His eyes saw the mangled bodies, wrecked and maimed by hidden mines, heard the screams and moans of once proud strong men. The familiar orders, shouted as problems arose, turned his stomach over and churned his thoughts.

Dave reflected that his first tour of duty abroad had turned him from a boy into a man. The four of them returned relatively unscathed, but wiser than their years. More tours were to follow, each one sucking out more energy and resilience than the last. The team spirit held out and grew as they faced and endured the challenges of yet another hostile country. They could not speak about what they had seen and experienced, to those dear to them. It would only cause worry and hurt. Only those experiencing the situation could understand, so they didn't bother to try and talk over what they felt or what they had been through. They closed up emotionally and mentally to all the pain and suffering they had witnessed or caused.

Nan had welcomed Dave home each time, listening but asking few questions. It was clear to him that she was deteriorating in health. He felt guilty that he had abandoned her so easily, though she never spoke of her disappointment. Her pleasure when he returned was obvious as she showered him with favourite meals. They reminisced over family memories, pored over photographs, and laughed over stupid experiences.

Bright lively eyes shone in her wrinkled face on those visits though Dave noticed how thin and frail she was becoming. Her resolve to do everything for herself was so important to her.

"Just let me get some help for you, it would make me feel happier if I knew you were ok," he pleaded.

"Don't fuss so, Dave, you know it gives me pleasure to look after myself. I'll let you know when I need something, I promise," she would reassure him each time. Reluctantly he would leave hoping that on his next visit he could make things safer. Informed by his superior officer of her death, though it was no surprise or shock, it hit him like a bolt and he fell apart.

The army flew him home immediately, and he went about the necessary organisation of her burial. A few distant relatives he hardly knew, stood along side him at the grave. He felt the familiar feeling of abandonment, as strong now as ever. Thirteen or twenty four years old the outcome was the same, he was left alone.

Sean, especially, stepped in and helped to cajole him out of his bereavement trough. He was always there, organising spare time, listening but giving no judgements. Working, parading a true comrade in arms, he became more like a brother. Sean became the rock that Dave needed. Gaz and Liam grew wary of interrupting this new development in their quartet. Still a vital part of the foursome, it wasn't long before Gaz's hint of jealousy began to be sensed. Army life was hectic though, and normality had to resume.

Dave knew that the fourth engagement to Afghanistan would be harder. Friendships still intact, he realised they had all changed, become wiser maybe, but a brittleness belied their strength. Dave had gone out on patrol that day, in much the same way as many times before. Alert but wary, he flicked his eyes to cover all the alleyways and buildings, aware of the position of his buddies, they aware of his post. The noises of gun shots exploding all around him, dust, heat and the whiteness of the sun scorched buildings overpowered him.

Dave slumped down aware of a small person in the doorway, trapped by events. His eyes met hers. She was small, with wide open eyes, a miniature of Sophie. At that moment the air around him exploded with an eruption of sound, catapulting him back and he heard the dreaded words 'man down'. A cacophony of voices rang out.

"Get down"

"Over there on the right"

"Help! Man down"

Glancing out he saw the body of Sean splayed in front of him. He had only taken his eyes off him for a second! How could he be down? Despite the air resounding with answering volleys of fire, Dave heard only silence. He rushed forward not caring, one of his four pillars, his brother, needed him. Spear heads of pain coursed through his legs, back and arm as the bomb exploded behind him, sending him soaring through the air.

He regained consciousness several hours later, and the stillness alarmed him. The dimly lit, sterile ward puzzled Dave. Struggling, he tried to clear his blurred vision and hazy thoughts. Like a bolt it hit him again, a body, Sean. He felt the plastering and bandages on himself with dismay, and wished he was with his friend. He was alone again.

They told him how lucky he was, several times, but Dave knew that he wasn't, he had failed.

"Call yourself my mate, you weren't there, again," the persistent inner voice repeated, "always missing when you're needed."

The remnants of the explosion had entered Dave's body in several places. They had successfully removed the shrapnel from all but one area. He would recover well, they were sure, and they would operate again on the final tiny piece of the shell, if needed. The small shard lodged inside him, Dave felt he deserved this reminder of how he had failed his friend and refused further surgery..

Repatriated back home, Dave did not make the recuperation they expected of him. Dissolving into uncontrollable fits of violence gave way to a profound depth in him that couldn't be reached. Post Traumatic Stress Disorder was the official prognosis, but Dave knew it was blame. Blame that couldn't be absolved

After his body had recovered to a reasonable state, they began to work on his mind . Months of treatment followed, but he made little progress. Dave could see the disappointment of the doctors around him, but he didn't care. He tried to respond but the more he tried the easier it was to slip away from their words and advice. What did they know? Their kindness didn't mitigate his self imposed verdict of blame. The drugs they prescribed cushioned him from reality, and he entered a twilight world of his own.

There he felt comfort in the numbness, and his pain would stop for a while until the drugs stopped working, returning the images of the dead and the living, Dad, Mum, Nan and Sophie whirling in and out of his nightmares. Sean alive and vibrant, battled with the image of his torn, lifeless, bloodied body. Escape from this spiral of torment seemed unobtainable. Gaz and Liam visited him frequently at first, eager to keep their friendship alive. Despite their words and offers of help, Dave was sure he could detect unspoken accusations in their eyes. They didn't need to say the words, he knew what they felt. He retreated further into sullen responses and bouts of anger they couldn't handle. Their visits became scarcer and shorter. Not long after, they were recalled to active duty, their assignments cut off the last thread between them and Dave.

Dave's discharge from the army seemed harsh but was inevitable. The transfer to medical treatment in civilian life was well organised. He was settled into accommodation and a support system set in motion. Regular psychiatric appointments were scheduled, and everything was done to provide a stable and caring situation in the community.

However, the professionals now around him had not considered the impact of any sight of army personnel or transport. These were an intrusion upon Dave's mental state. He had only to glimpse an army uniform and Sean flew into view, his listless eyes staring at him accusatorily, and the downward cycle would begin again.

In his more lucid moments Dave began to realise that he must get away. Somewhere there must be a place where the quietness he craved could be found. So taking his few belongings that had no connection with his past life, he slipped away, out of the system of support where no one would recognise or know his shame. Pay books, photos, army records were abandoned in his room, to be found by anxious army and medical personnel. Contact was cut. He took only the cash saved and packed the clothes he could carry.

Over the following months a pattern began to shape in Dave's life. He had left with the outward appearance of a clean, healthy young man. His state of mind disguised and camouflaged by the prescribed drugs he was taking. The first task on entering any new town was to register with a doctor and maintain his supply of medicines. He became adept at building a web of lies around his past circumstances and his current living arrangements. He used his money sparingly on cheap living accommodation, frequented pubs and struck up drinking acquaintances. It wasn't difficult to bum a night or two at their place and feed himself cheaply at their expense.

As his cash dwindled, he resorted to any method, such as using hostels, or tricking hoteliers and slipping away early to avoid paying up. When anyone questioned him in an effort to help, which annoyed him intensely, he evaded their persistent enquiries. As, inevitably, they began to get closer to the truth, he would judge he needed to move on again.

His progress around the country, travelling from town to town, was laboured. Hitch hiking and walking mile after mile drew on his army training and resourcefulness. Dave's mind still causing him to have sleepless nights, nightmares and panic attacks increased his problems without outside aid. He began to look like an itinerant, unshaved and neglected.

He kept out of the country villages; he was too obvious and easily noticed in small communities, standing out as a stranger. Towns were easier to melt into the background, without interrogation. From time to time he took odd jobs, when he was lucky enough, supplementing his pot of cash.

His downward spiral of hopelessness went unnoticed as in a constant fog of drink and drugs he faced his inner conflicts. When his cash finally ran out, Dave began to call on whatever charities he could find for help. Begging was no longer beneath him, he had no pride. Hot meals and handouts were accepted, with the thought that he would find a better way, but always tomorrow!

Occasionally church members would intervene, always with the sincerest of intentions, but they needed too much information for Dave. He had no desire to rake up his past, secure in a strange way to his new routine. Sleeping rough in the summer was acceptable for Dave, he didn't have to explain himself. In the winter harshness he would take any help offered, but only as a last resort.

Mile by mile, imperceptibly, Dave was returning to his birthplace without mentally recognising his target. Ten years of rough sleeping and isolation. The tree and park where he had played football with his father, congregated with school mates, met with Sophie, was now his resting place. The familiar scene, unchanged for

Dave, helped him forget the horrors he had seen, it allowed him to rest and gave him peace. However hard the bench was under the Sycamore tree, the comfort it provided was as wonderful as any bed.

Unaware that the tree was condemned, he had become reliant upon it.

Like a light murmuring wind the despair of Dave hung around the tree, on his departure, invisible but detectable. The Sycamore tree that had provided succour and rest overnight, now absorbed the remnants of hopelessness. It could withstand the changes of the seasons, but was helpless against the emotional turmoil of humans who used its protection.

It had stood unnoticed and unappreciated for decades of years. Drawing in breath alongside generations of people. It imbibed the colour and complexities of the time into its very core, just as it accommodated the rain, wind and sun that beat down incessantly on its canopy, trunk and roots.

Many would be overwhelmed with the myriad stories it could have repeated, but incredulous to the ethos of a living plant soaking up the unseen tendrils of human emotion. A small step for us to take, to compare the empathy of animals to pain and suffering which connects with humans and helps recovery.

Dave's black depression hung over him like cumulus clouds scudding across his thoughts as in the sky above. He anticipated a downpour of events with few silver linings, just as the tree waited for the changes in atmosphere heralding the storm to come.

Chapter 2

7.00 a.m.

Across the park, jogging alongside his spaniel Fern, Bob anticipated the day with pleasure. He stopped under the tree to take a welcome break, he wasn't as fit as he used to be. Today he would be meeting the buyer and manager of a chain of toy shops. His business might expand if he could sell his ideas. Bob wasn't good at convincing people with words, he only hoped that the sample would speak for itself. His fingers touched the etching on the tree of familiar initials. There, entwined together alongside many other carvings, were BS and SR, his name together with Sophie his wife.

Casting back he recalled the day they had done this.

"Sophie, why did you come out with me?" Bob had asked fearfully.

He knew she had felt bad about lying to Dave.

"You're such a fool, you make me laugh, who could resist that?" she had answered. She had convinced herself it would do no harm just one date with him. She liked Dave. He was so sensitive, she had felt the urge to protect him, but Bob was so different. She knew the gossip around school and witnessed the teacher's nightmares with his clowning antics. Still, he brought out a bubble of joy deep within her. Laugh after laugh enticed her towards Bob; little by little, despite her misgivings, she came alive in his company. Loyalty to Dave gave way to the magnetic field of Bob.

"Bob, do you think Dave will be alright with us?" she questioned.

"I don't see how we can ease his feelings, but it's not right to stay with him just for that, is it?" he reasoned.

Doubtfully, Sophie had shaken her head, not convinced but strangely certain that there was no other way. He changed the subject.

"Sophie, I want us to carve our initials on this tree, just look at all these names, I bet I could do just as well."

"Do you think all these are from sweethearts?" she pondered, "let's make it a sign for us".

"What do you mean?" Bob was starting to doubt his idea.

"Well, if you can carve it with just your penknife and it stays there for a month without anyone messing it up, then we'll know we should be together."

Bob fingered the small penknife given to him by his grandfather. He always carried it with him, reminding him of the hours he had spent watching the older man whittle away at wooden figures.

Not one to flinch from a challenge, but aware of his limitations, especially with the small blade, he began his mission. The result was there for all to see, and though he still felt tinges of regret, he knew that they had been true to their hearts. Time had proved them correct, for now they appeared to be the perfect married couple. Mindful of the journey that their ten year marriage had taken, Bob was fully aware of their bumpy ride. Two children later, he felt smug satisfaction that, for the moment, their life was opening up for them.

Sophie and he had had a rocky start. Bob's family gelled immediately with her; she was the antithesis of himself. He had drifted through senior school with few aims or ambitions. Always the clown of the class, he succeeded in finding himself in the corridor or outside the headmaster's room too often. Between disjointed lessons and disregarded homework he lagged behind. This gave him further excuses. To avoid feeling a failure it was easier if he never tried. He limped through the later years of school, popular but always in trouble, both at school and at home.

The situation was made worse by the circumstances of his home life.

"Bob, we've another call from school to come in and see them," his mother would say despairingly, "what's wrong now?"

"Can't stop now Mum, I'll be late," he would call out, one foot already out of the door. He would square it with the head of year, try and deflect the need for parents and teachers to get together, he thought as he sped away. Later that night the inevitable words from his dad would interrupt his scheming.

"What's wrong with you, how much longer before you begin to grow up?"

"Fooling around won't put butter on your bread."

He knew the words off by heart, in fact the imaginary sketch he mimicked to his friends was a favourite past time. Busy parents were annoyed and disappointed at the distractions and worries that he was causing them. His two older brothers had conformed to some normal pattern. They weren't saints by any means, but behaved at school, and were now settled in comfortable careers. Bob could remember the surprise of the teachers who knew them.

"Bob Saunders, are you related to Tony and James?" they questioned.

"I can't say you look like them, but we'll find out what you're about, shall we?"

They weighed him up alongside his brothers, and found him wanting. He didn't care, he had no need for stupid subjects or exams and qualifications. It wasn't cool to like lessons or behave in class, homework became a challenge. How many different reasons could you find to excuse yourself?

Sophie, however, blossomed at school, and honestly enjoyed the chosen subjects which would lead to her ambition of becoming a nurse. Bob had noticed her with Dave, smiling and listening to his ideas. They were all part of a larger group and it was only natural that he sometimes found himself in her company. He suppressed inwardly his friendship with Dave. Though Dave had been a special friend for Bob, he had a quiet aura in contrast to the extrovert nature of himself. Bob respected Dave in sport and aspired to be more sensitive when dealing with others, as his friend showed so many times. It was noticeable that Sophie was encouraging his confidence and Dave was flowering into a stronger person. Struggling with his attraction for Sophie, Bob still manoeuvred and schemed that these accidental meetings became more frequent. Asking her out was a natural consequence, and it came as a shock to him when she accepted. He pushed these awkward thoughts to one side as he had done at the time. They were a pair, well suited for each other. Hadn't he proved that? He jogged on again, the spaniel eager to run pulling on the lead.

Their history resurfaced again in his thoughts and he couldn't stop dwelling on their past. They had married hurriedly with both families' acceptance and anxious thoughts hidden away. The baby had been a disturbing interruption in their immature dreams. Bob liked to think he had cushioned Sophie from her parents' disapproval at this mistake. In truth he had only compounded their worries. He was jobless and reliant on his own parents. How could he take care of himself, let alone a wife and child? Was he work shy? They knew his sense of humour and though they warmed towards his personality, he was still an unknown quantity. They were used to a conventional working background with strong work ethics. Did Bob fit into this adult life he was entering? Sophie's parents worried and struggled with the thought of their future together. Sophie had been so unsure of events and what to do. Bob and she had long painful and honest talks, lasting late into the night. After much consideration, they decided they would keep the baby and marry. It didn't matter that they were young and had past liaisons, they loved each other .

Together they moved into a small flat only two months before the birth of their son. Both sets of parents had helped to set up the place. Bob had learnt to decorate and even managed to replace the old carpets with cleaner laminate flooring. It was the first sign of his initiative and drive as he handled the wooden boards. He remembered his dad's words with gratitude.

"Here's the money, go and get whatever suits you for the flooring. We can't have your first child living in a dirty place." The novelty of finding pleasure with what he'd done was new to him.

"Look, Sophie, do you think it's OK, will it do?" he waited quietly for her reaction, unsure of his skill. Sophie marvelled at his efforts and encouraged him further. It was a good feeling to achieve what they wanted together.

Bob had been told by his parents that now he had to shoulder the responsibilities of a husband and father. He made a pact with himself that he wouldn't ask either of their parents for help if he could find any other way. Occasionally he found odd jobs to do in the area, but the money was poor and barely paid for their bills. Labouring work always seemed to be outside the area and he needed to be around for Sophie and the baby.

Christmas seemed to be the catalyst for propelling him into action. They had no spare money for presents for the family. Sophie set about knitting and making things from extra material her mum had thrown out. Bob had no skills so he tussled at how he could make any contribution. Sophie's younger sister had longed for a doll's house for some time. She had played at her friend's home and spent hours opening and shutting doors and windows and moving the tiny furniture around. When Bob passed the joinery shop an idea flew into his head that might be possible. Piled up in a heap outside were oddments of wood. Small off cuts from larger projects the firm was undertaking. He hesitated for a moment then pushing nerves to one side, walked into the office. Fumbling for the exact words, he muttered,

"Sorry to bother you, but I noticed some bits of wood, do you need them?" The burly man nearby, eyeing him suspiciously, grunted that he could have as many as he liked and returned to his work. Satisfied with his cumbersome trophy, he triumphantly brought the pieces of wood back to show his wife.

To her credit Sophie had not doubted his plan when he gabbled out his intentions, even though she might have had many misgivings. Bob loved the feel of wood, its textures, grain and colour. He had surreptitiously watched in the wood work classes, not appearing to be interested. At home he tried out what he had seen in secret. You could learn a lot if you listened and watched, he realised. He was talented, undetected by himself and completely unobserved by others. His grandfather's joinery tools were left in dad's shed since his death, so Bob gathered them up to practice. His parents' surprise at the request to use them, gave way to relief that he was busy at last.

The little doll's house was simple but precisely put together, a true work of love. Once started he had beavered away. Mistakes were made but eagerly rectified. No one could interrupt this venture, totally engrossed, he couldn't stop until it was finished. He and Sophie agreed it was the perfect gift for Kate. A coat of paint and it would be ready for the wrapping paper. The delight with the present was evident on Kate's small face, but to Bobs surprise the whole family praised and congratulated him over and over. It seemed ridiculous that this doll's house should gain him such admiration when he found it so easy to do. Bob basked in the glory. For once he'd done something to make his family proud. Pride gave way though, as his mind flew randomly to an old feeling that wasn't helpful and in complete contrast.

"Proud of yourself?" his inner voice taunted. "Family, wife and son, you've got it all. You don't need friends, but I did."

It might have been Dave's words Bob felt the familiar disgust at his betrayal. He could persuade himself he was only young, but lying and cheating were the same whatever your age. Dave hadn't deserved that treatment from him, and now he couldn't make it right. He had made attempts to explain, only to be rejected. In no time Dave had disappeared from the neighbourhood, and Bob had heard of his enlistment into the army from other school mates. He resolved that he would make it right, but how and when? It would have to wait. The birth of their son, Peter, occupied Bob and Sophie totally over the following weeks. Tired but gloriously happy they struggled along, becoming a stable family. Bob had promised Kate that he would make her some furniture for her doll's house, if she was patient. Childlike, she had asked each time she visited, if he had something for her. He couldn't disappoint her again. So, in-between baby routines and work schedules, he spirited himself away with his precious wood. The patience and diligence of his skilled hands began to produce miniature tables, chairs and beds. Lovingly crafted, glued together and painted they stood as a testament to his perseverance.

Sophie was so thrilled, she had to show her mother.

"Mum, what do you think of these?"

"Where did you buy them, Sophie?" she queried, "they're really lovely, and so perfect for the doll's house. I thought it would take for ever to find a shop selling furniture for it."

"I didn't buy them, Bob made them," she triumphantly replied.

As she and her mother inspected and fingered the items they realised that Bob's innate talent had been found. It was his mother-in-law that added to his luck though. She had searched for a small doll of the right size to complete the toy house. It wasn't so easy to find one in scale with the doll's house, but a small back street revealed a likely shop. Tucked between two smart retailers, the window of the store attracted those people searching for the more unusual playthings or games.

Sophie's mum, Helen, knew she had to get the doll exactly right so she tucked the little chair and table into her bag to test out its suitability for a prospective doll. The small table and chair were expertly crafted, detailed and lovingly smoothed for any child to touch. The joints were unobtrusive, and a light varnish gave them a real feeling of matching full size models.

Entering the shop she tentatively unwrapped the items, one by one, to a patient proprietor.

"I'm looking for a doll that would fit this furniture, "she queried, "but also, I was wondering if you might be interested in these?" she paused, "do you think you could use them?"

He inspected each one, turning them in his hands and feeling the workmanship. It seemed a lifetime before he spoke.

"These are remarkable, my dear, where did you get them?"

She gave him the details about Bob, careful not to appear over eager or divulge the family connection. She thought the samples would speak for themselves.

"I think this bespoke furniture might become heirlooms of the future. I've never seen better!"

The toy shop owner and Helen were of one mind, he ought to see the whole house as he was bowled over by the quality of the little chair and table. She dived back home to fetch it. Once he had seen the complete toy she could tell he recognised the potential for his business.

Eagerly she returned home, worried as to how she could pass on the information to Bob without alerting his usual wariness. She needn't have been so anxious she reflected. Both Sophie and Bob had learned the hard way, to take any opportunity that came their way.

To his surprise Bob found the shop keeper so supportive of his work that he was eager to show him all he could do. This first venture of one unit of a doll's house and furniture was to give him the foothold into making money. Better still it wasn't a drudge, more like a hobby that he couldn't wait to follow. He was intent on making money to support the three of them, so casual work had to come first. It was a second piece of luck that helped him further. Still using the wood off-cuts from the local joinery firm, Bob became a regular visitor in order to watch and learn how they handled the wood. Soon he began to help in an unofficial capacity and as the joinery company took on urgent jobs, he was asked to help as a casual paid employee.

A regular income for the home made life so much easier. Bob, meanwhile, used every spare moment to work on other doll's houses and contents. Sophie, after the first months of motherhood, saw that she needed to support Bob in such a way that he could focus on the new venture. It was satisfying to watch the mini house take form and shape and they made plans together. How to turn their dreams into reality was the question. As she found that the evenings became lonely with Bob so busy, she returned to her personal dream of becoming a nurse. How could she make this happen? She knew she must find a way.

Together they delivered the completed toy house to the shop. It was displayed in a central position in the window to show its full beauty and workmanship. Over the next few months Bob worked hard to hone his wood working skills. A second and third order for similar toy houses was placed by the original shop keeper. It seemed that word of mouth promoted both the shop, and craftsman. Bob began to wonder how he could fulfil these orders as he worked tirelessly each day, week and month. He had many other ideas to diversify and extend his business. Rocking horses, dolls cradles, castles and forts were designed, a prototype made and as these were accepted, were added to the list of orders waiting.

Peter crawled forward, Bob's parents melted in adoration of their grandson. The flat was bulging at the seams now, with baby paraphernalia, household debris and wooden objects in various stages of assembly.

"You need to keep everything higher," Sophie's mum suggested." It won't be long before he'll find trouble, little hands love to explore."

The baby worship continued and, in the laughing atmosphere, Bob was ushered aside by his dad.

"Why don't you find a workshop, it would make your life so much easier?"

"Can't do it yet dad, orders are coming in but we're strapped for cash. It will have to wait. We're lucky, I can use the spare bedroom," he added.

"Look, don't wait, I know of a small place that might suit your needs," his dad carefully suggested. "It might solve your space problems and you can pay the loan back later."

It was the answer to Bob's worries. Pushing aside any qualms at accepting help from his dad he reluctantly but gratefully thanked his parents. The relief at a problem solved now spurred him on to survey the small workroom where he could spread out and work on multiple elements of the project. It seemed that all the pieces of the business were fitting together like a jigsaw. As the weeks turned into months, and the months into years, the business grew and prospered. The shop keeper, in tandem with Bob, promoted the houses and furniture over the internet. Discerning customers and specialised outlets began to relay their satisfaction, generating more orders. It was obvious that Bob needed help. His paid work at the joinery company could not be sustained, so he reluctantly left his mates. In trepidation he began to expand on his own, and employed two young recruits from his old school. In time the number he employed grew and grew. For the first time Bob could pass on his own enthusiasm and skills, motivating them to enjoy their work.

Sophie worked hard, helping with the administrative side of their business but additionally, had organised her own nursing studies, as their son Pete grew older. The couple became known for their hard work and perseverance, and a second child, a daughter they named Jane, completed their happiness.

Worries and problems came and were solved as they moved to larger premises to employ more staff and meet growing orders. Bob's parents were amazed at how he shouldered the new responsibilities. They admitted to each other privately that their worries for his future seemed now to be unfounded. Bob basked in this new respect for him. Though he always knew his parents loved him, he recalled how he had wanted to shock them. The youngest of a trio, he had fought to be different from his brothers. It wasn't that he wanted to be competitive, only he hated the idea of conforming to a family mould.

Sophie and he grew alongside the two children learning the skills of parenting as each new problem arose. He had become so vigilant at protecting his own children, the habit extended to any risk situation. It was usual for him to drop off Peter and Jane some days to their schools, helping Sophie to begin her morning. One particular morning he was alarmed to see a small girl banging her forehead on the wall outside a door to the community centre where a playgroup met. It seemed to be deserted with no one around to intervene. The little girl was wailing, blood streamed down her face, but she continued in this way without a pause. He couldn't bear to watch and acted without any hesitation to stop the distress to both the child and himself. He knelt near her blocking the wall from her small body.

A distraught mother bolted through the door and quickly scooped up her weeping daughter. Explanations and thanks were flung out as she comforted little Melanie, handing over the child's tambourine which seemed to be the cause of the bother and calm her down. Bob never really understood the whole scene he'd just witnessed, the mother's embarrassment was obvious and he excused himself as soon as possible to relieve any further awkwardness. He was just glad to be of some help, but even now he remembered hoping that someone would be there, if needed, for his children.

Sophie, with the help of her mother, had juggled precious time to study nursing. Diligent and dedicated, she flew through the theory and knew the practical elements were ideal for her. The shift schedule helped as Bob and she swapped the parenting duties in the evening. This allowed a precious slot of time for Bob to plan his business after the kids were in bed. Pete, their son, now approaching the end of junior school, was a tough, athletic sports fanatic. His blond hair and height stood out on the football pitch as he sprinted and raced for the ball. Jane was a precise copy of her mother, her eyes, hair and build so like Sophie. The pride of watching the two children grow spurred Bob on to be the best dad he could be.

Approaching the end of the walk, the spaniel, less frenetic, had calmed down to a fast walking pace. Bob remembered his need to get home urgently.

"Come on, Fern, it's late," he tugged at the lead.

"I need a shower and breakfast, there's not much time." This special day beckoned him. He must calm himself down, look in at the works and make sure everyone knew what to do. Then collect his notes and samples before heading off for his meeting. He must succeed and make the contract profitable. After all, he had more than his mouth to feed, or that of his family. Others were relying on him too.

Anticipation hung in the air as Bob hurried away, just as in the tree birds sang melodiously one to another. The thrust of this new day was apparent in the park, insects buzzing around, creatures searching for food. They mirrored the ambition and drive of Bob.

The tree, strong, reliable and grounded had roots curling and sourcing nourishment in all directions. Bob, it could be argued, had learnt lessons from its systems, to establish strong foundations. He had come a long way from the fun loving, unreliable youth to the man he was today.

However he wanted to emulate what the tree stood for, to show he was constant, consistent but most of all had foundations. The tree had withstood drought, storms and gales surviving against all odds. So could he and his business.

Chapter 3

Dave

Dave painfully hobbled onwards as he moved his leg carefully from the overnight cramps of the night on the bench. He needed a hot drink to fully restore warmth into his limbs, and searched in his dull mind where to find it. As he walked along the streets he fondly recalled the steaming hot mugs of tea and wedges of bread buttered by the nuns. Convents found in some towns often made provision for tramps and itinerants, without protest or judgement. No such luck here though, the nearest convent was many miles away.

He was aware of a small number of coins hidden in an inside pocket, but didn't want to use them so early in the day. He would need them so he could afford the luxury to clean himself up. A small kiosk on the corner of two large intersecting roads would be his first call today. He had struck up a loose friendship with the operator of this van, and, occasionally, was given a free drink and any stale sandwich left over from the day before. Mindful that he didn't abuse this source, he left two or three days between his visits. Today he was in luck, the van wasn't busy and the man seeing him approach waved him over. Two old sandwiches and a hot mug of sweet tea safely inside him, Dave felt the familiar relief in his gut and warm appreciation for another human.

He thanked him earnestly and gathering up the energy for this new day, he wandered away planning the next few hours.

Chapter 4

9.00 a.m.

All around the park signals of the awakening households, the increase of traffic, and the insistence of the new day had begun. For the last two hours people had drifted off to work. The busy urban hour grew pace and intensity towards the magical hour of nine o 'clock. Church bells peeling, the school gates closed by a determined teacher as the last disappearing heels of a latecomer ran through the entrance door.

Stranded like whales, a gaggle of mothers, babies and toddlers were beached behind the green iron bars. The park, within sight of this primary school, beckoned as a welcome haven from the preceding two hours. Settled under the shady canopy of leaves they parked their prams and pushchairs. Toddlers happily played on the swings and slides as at last the young mothers could grab a minute for themselves.

"Hi, glad to see you, I've got something here that might help Billy to sleep," Susie pulled out a night light from her bag. Hazel, covering up the tiny infant in the push chair, cast her tired eyes towards the voice with a weary smile.

"Thanks, Susie, you're a pal."

"Are you able to come with me next Tuesday, Hazel?" asked another mum as she struggled to contain the wriggling toddler under her arms. The swings enticed him though he was hardly able to walk.

A random support group had emerged in their midst over the weeks. Laughter and woes in equal measure. Single mums could feel the unspoken support of their companions. Family problems and unemployment issues could be voiced and solutions proffered. It was an antidote for the loneliness and isolation they felt whilst caring for their babies. Guilty of these negative emotions that motherhood had given them, it was a welcome relief to find others feeling the same way. Conversations that didn't have the perpetual 'why' oiled their minds. Explanations were not needed.

Into this little group Emma had appeared, unexpectedly, one day. A thin slip of a creature, she had followed them from the school gates with her youngest child, Tina. Over a period of time she had watched them wistfully, but it was her eldest child David who drew her into their circle. He had slowly made friends with Andrew the son of Susie. Mother and son rapidly drew them into the group, born extroverts they knew no other way. As Emma gravitated towards Sue, no one noticed how little she had to say in the larger group. She listened and watched, giving few clues to her background or life. It was clear that she thoroughly enjoyed the time and visibly relaxed in their company. If they had watched more carefully, they might have noticed her quick intermittent glances around the park. They might have observed the wariness in any questions she was forced to answer about herself, but large groups absorb the natural quiet members and she was known as a listener.

Susie, in contrast, knew and mixed with everyone. A fun loving person, she seemed to bring out the best in all she met. It might be assumed that someone so involved with the social chit-chat would be too busy to take in details. However, born into a large family, she was a practiced exponent of sensing out moods or problems. Emma both fascinated and puzzled Susie but, as the meetings progressed, she began to read her better. Never giving many clues away, Emma had times when she seemed more jittery than others. It was amusing that she felt the cold so badly, and they teased her gently about this. In the summer heat she was always covered up and they put this down to how skinny she was, privately envying her slim figure.

Surprisingly, for a determined Susie, it had taken many attempts to draw from Emma that she was married to Kevin. They had married at a young age and Kevin supported them working as a driver for the local supermarket. This accounted for Emma's reluctance to go along to the shops with anyone. There was no need, she must be well supplied daily on Kevin's return. Sometimes Emma would confide in Susie how seldom she went anywhere. Her children certainly had to be bribed and coaxed to play, preferring to stay close by their mother's side.

"There's an offer on at the precinct supermarket," a proud mum would inform everyone, "you get cash off your next shop."

"I could use that, thanks, Jane."

"Do you fancy a coffee there Emma?" Susie enquired.

We don't need any food and I do have chores to do, so maybe next time," Emma stuttered," I don't want to wind Kev up, he has a lot to worry about." Susie repeatedly gave Emma invitations to join or visit them, but they were always refused with feeble excuses.

Emma had once admitted that Kevin was difficult if she went against his wishes. Family life was enough for him, and he wanted his children and wife to enjoy time together. A perfect unit of four, for him, they didn't need any others.

"Emma, it would help your children if they had time out of school to mix with others," Susie had argued.

"I can't Susie, we're ok and Kev's taking us out anyway," Emma reasoned.

"Face facts, Emma, even if you're content, it's not right for the children to suffer," Susie persisted in her blunt direct manner.

"What do you know about it, Susie?" Emma flared up, her face reddening, "my children are well looked after."

"I still think you might enjoy a trip out sometime Emma, I wasn't blaming anyone," Susie attempted to cool the words down. Several pairs of eyes flicked between the two of them.

"Kev really tries to be a good husband and father, and we do go out together," Emma's voice trailed off as she realised that she was the centre of attention.

A pause in the squabble gave way to more awkward minutes until a toddler's cries brought them back to earth. Normality was resumed and no more was said by Susie, though it was obvious to her that Emma needed help.

Several times, a chance remark from a group member would make Emma clam up further. Worse still she would scuttle away early, despite voices begging her to stay. Some of the women became exasperated at her reactions, others gave up, shrugging off any problems she might have.

"How can anyone help? She's just so blinkered," one protested.

"Perhaps if she spoke more about her problems someone could do something," suggested a second. No one confronted her, but passed her over as impossible to help.

Over the many gatherings Susie maintained her friendship with Emma, seeking an occasion to let Emma confide. The signs were there of her unhappiness, but Emma covered them up, giving no clues if she could to anyone. Swollen eyes that were bright from prolonged crying, the sweeping orbit of her eyes over her surroundings as if anticipating trouble, were familiar habits. Once, Susie glimpsed an old scar on Emma's arm as the cardigan wrinkled up unexpectedly before it was hastily pulled down.

Today, Emma seemed more distracted than usual as the gaggle of voices swirled above her head. Tina wouldn't leave her to play on the swings, and she seemed to tremble in rhythm with her mother's body. Susie was worried. Was this the day she might be of some use? Emma was rocking Tina nervously, her eyes focused somewhere in the distance. She was back in time to her own childhood in a rowdy family of five. As the eldest, she had adored her twin brothers when they were born four years after her. Family life was exhausting but generally light and amusing.

A blip came as a teenager, when adjusting to the social mix of boys of her age. The crush she felt for Dave, two years older than her had, fortunately, not been recognised by him or anyone. He was far too intent on his mates to notice her. The local gossips had told her of the deaths of his parents, but this only made him more attractive. His sensitive nature brought out a nurturing instinct in her. Shy and apprehensive of any fun made of her, she kept secret in her heart this unrequited love.

Sixteen approached all too soon, and she struggled to know what she wanted to do as a career. Hairdressing vacancies were posted up at school and she applied for her training. Content in this work, she began to emerge into a more confident young woman. Learning of her parents' dream to emigrate to Australia posed a real dilemma for her. She really loved what she was doing and now had a circle of friends around her that she would miss. On the horizon she had dreams of her own. Then Kevin had entered her life.

"Hello there, can I make an appointment?" he had asked as he came into the salon.

Emma had smiled, trying not to take a second look until the date and time was completed on the screen.

"Great, that's fine," he continued, "I'll look forward to meeting up, perhaps I'll be lucky enough to get you for the cut. Do you think you could squeeze me in?" She had blushed secretly thinking that she'd reschedule any competing appointments.

Kevin was smaller than the average build, but still quite a striking figure none the less. He was always aware of his image, some might have thought him vain, but Emma put it down to current fashion trends and his wish to follow cutting edge styles. He was five years older than her and courted her with more imagination than younger men.

Spontaneous outings and surprises showered down on Emma, and she felt extra special in his company. He was really good at organising their time together and soon infiltrated her home and met the family. The light breeze that might have first epitomised Kevin's attention and focus, soon became more insistent. His strength and purpose overwhelmed her young mind as the hurricane gained strength. Emma experienced a protectiveness and care never found outside her parents' love. During these first few months she was totally sucked up in the vortex of their ardour. Compliant, she wanted to please and return his attention.

Emma's parents were, at first, a little wary of this gale that was sweeping into their lives. They could see how dependant Emma had become to Kevin and as he wooed her they too fell under his spell. Plans for their departure drew nearer and they were caught up in the million and one jobs to be completed. Most of their extended family were already settled in Australia, so many of their potential problems became easier to iron out. Emma's brothers were excited at the prospects the country would offer them and had no reluctance to wave goodbye to their friends. They had each other and the bond between twins generally supported all new ventures.

Months were passing and the date for leaving England grew steadily nearer. Emma worried and chewed over what decision to make. She loved her family and, still immature in many ways, she couldn't think of a life without them. Kevin would talk and talk with her until her head span with all the ideas and questions.

"Do you think you can easily carry on your hairdressing training in Australia?"

"What about where you live, will it be a city, town or village?"

"If you can't get a work visa for months, what will you do with your time?"

Kevin became a support to her prevarications, he used up all her spare time after work. Her head full of the implications of her choice, she had no time to think, isolate herself or take counsel from her friends. Time with her pals had become limited and she was losing the threads of their companionship. Finally, her father, realising that the options might be too hard for Emma, suggested an interim alternative.

"Look, Emma, don't get into a panic, we can find a solution," her dad explained, "stay here for a month or so and feel if it's right for you."

"But, Dad, I don't know if that would be right, I know I'm going to miss you all," Emma would cry.

"What about this then? Stay here and finish your training year, then follow us out there. You'll be clearer then, if it is to be a holiday or if you want to join us," her dad proposed. Calculating that Emma would miss her mother, he reasoned that a year of independence would work in their favour. He hadn't reckoned on Kevin's innate ability to seize the chance. The proposal of marriage seemed the perfect solution. Emma glowed with the idea of becoming Kevin's wife. It seemed perfect, the next step was an obvious outcome of their love. If her parents were dismayed at leaving their eldest behind, this dissipated at the suggestion that the newly wedded couple would join them. Kevin assured them that they would save and plan for a future in Australia. He had no family to hold him back in England, so no difficult choices would hinder them. Kevin had showed how committed and loving a man he was towards Emma. They were happy and relieved to give their blessing.

The small wedding, planned to the last detail by Kevin, took place one week before the family left for Australia. Emma's parents, rather relieved that the event was taken over so efficiently, relaxed and finished off the numerous jobs still hanging over them. It was a tearful Emma who waved goodbye to her parents and brothers at the airport. No amount of internal reasoning, could give her peace as she missed them each day. She told herself repeatedly that she would meet up soon. She phoned and wrote regularly, but couldn't replace their hugs or familiar contact.

Settling into her new flat with Kevin, took some of the pain away.

"Emma can you make time to get the colour charts after work?" he called out as he flew out of the door.

"Emma, where are the tools I asked you to get?"

"Have you forgotten those jobs I asked you to do?" an exasperated voice would repeat. She had so much to do. The perfection Kevin wanted in his home appeared over zealous to her, but she complied. They cleaned and decorated each room, making the final result a little palace. Choosing materials and paint had been a revelation, so intense was the involvement of Kevin. Generally, it became Kevin's choice and she agreed that he had a flair for design and texture. She began to wonder though at the expense of it all; it seemed extravagant if it was to last for only a year. His obsession for tidiness became more apparent with each day together.

"Can you tidy up the food cupboard, Emma, I can't see what I need to bring home for us?" he demanded.

"Must you leave the towels wet? Put them away," he ordered.

It was easier for her to adjust she reasoned as she hated confrontations. So she listened and trained herself to follow his wishes. Cupboards were inspected for order and system, shelves reorganised several times. The linen was washed so regularly, the machine might have waved a white flag in surrender. Emma would hide an inner smile at the absurdity of the regime.

The pleasure she felt when he praised her efforts more than rewarded her. She loved him completely and their new life helped to compensate for the separation from her family. The friends from her former life seemed busy now and in a circle of their own. Surprised at how little spare time she had, she realised that work and home had consumed her new life. Occasionally she made arrangements with friends at the salon, but it amazed her that she always clashed with tickets bought by Kevin on the same day.

"I've bought tickets for that film we wanted to see," Kevin pouted, "are your friends more important than us?"

It never worked out to keep her plan, and it was better to cancel her meeting with her pals than risk a fuss. In those early years Kevin would bring home unexpected gifts or flowers which thrilled her. He would arrange a trip or weekend away without asking her. His surprises were so frequent she lapped them up and felt so lucky. Sometimes she would suggest a place she might like to go, but it never seemed to happen. She knew she was foolish in her ideas, so slowly she pushed them aside, fearing ridicule or negative comments. It didn't occur to her that the whole diary of their days was planned by Kevin, and he was only happy if events were entirely on his terms.

Emma's pregnancy and months leading up to the birth of their son dented the hero worship she normally spent on her husband. Inevitably his words would puncture her bubble.

"Surely, you don't have to keep that clinic appointment. Can't you reschedule? I'll take time off work," he insisted. Kevin felt the loss of her complete focus on him, and he wasn't able to dictate her movements. Regular clinics and prenatal appointments gave a space for her to meet women in similar circumstances.

His childish bouts and tantrums became a consistent pattern which she heartily disliked. Though it wasn't worth arguing back, she began to see a side of him that wasn't likeable. Periods of silence for days on end were a relief, she had to concede. However, the sulks would continue unless she apologised and confessed to her part in why their relationship was strained.

"Kev, you know I love you. I'll try not to do it again, you're right I am to blame," she pushed aside her disloyal thoughts. Using all her tactics to placate his mood, he would at last come out of his intractable stance. Emma was sure that Kevin wanted the child. In truth, the knowledge of the conception had come at a time when plans for emigrating to Australia seemed to be coming together. She had saved hard and, with the growing insistence of her father, had pressed home the plans they had made for joining the family.

"I've managed to save more this month with the tips I get. We should have enough put by for our tickets soon," she told him excitedly.

He had barely looked up, but later had spent his earnings on an expensive bracelet for her. She knew he wanted to show his love for her and the child they were expecting. Emma had pushed aside suspicious thoughts that popped up in her mind. She was certain that she had taken her contraceptive pills. Her confusion at conceiving transferred to genuine surprise and delight at the baby growing inside her.

Kevin had been really happy but, sensible as always, he concluded that a birth at home in the UK would be the best idea. Emma would have the support of her own doctor and the child would have a British Passport, possibly later dual nationality. Emma understood that his thoughtfulness was for her good, but nagging disappointment that her mother would not be with her at the birth still clouded her mind. Their son arrived safely and Emma's pleasure at this new life was soon marred by trivial demands that Kevin insisted upon. Once away from the influence of the nurses and doctors, he took control. Feeding, bathing, sleeping were all put under tight constraints of his regime. Studying endless piles of books and articles on child rearing, though laudable in Emma's eyes, became fodder for Kevin's endless dictates.

Naming the baby was the one highlight in the darkness of this programme. Kevin had inadvertently chosen the name David for his son, after a distant uncle in his own family, without the knowledge of Emma's first infatuation. Smiling inwardly, she cherished her girlish dream and thought that the name David suited her boy really well.

Little David soon began to assert himself and Emma would have loved to have had the freedom to adapt and change the routine to suit both of them. Kevin made sure this didn't happen. He had taken to arriving home unexpectedly during the day time. These unpredictable visits allowed him to check up that his orders were being followed. Emma hoped that his work would limit his flexibility, but he managed to squeeze in time between driving from outlet to outlet. The random nature of his appearance began to make her nervous. She began to dread the sound of the van and squeak of the door opening.

Regular health visitors had been spurned by Kevin in favour of Emma attending her own doctor's clinics. These appointments never fitted in for Kevin and, as it was only fair that they should both be involved with bringing up their son, they were changed. It might be supposed that Emma's parents would have noticed the change in their daughter, but a distance of so many miles easily allowed the relationships to take on a superficiality. Emma became proficient at disguising her unhappiness. She didn't want to worry them. How could they help anyway? She needed to get herself healthy then maybe they could go ahead and join them in Australia.

The confidence of Emma plummeted lower and lower, as even the baby seemed to cry more. She nursed and comforted him but he didn't respond quickly enough for Kevin. He blamed Emma's inadequacies for lacking simple mothering skills.

"What's wrong with you, why can't you find out why he's crying?" he demanded.

"You're always tired, anyone would think you gave birth to twins."

As he shouted and screamed at her the tension in the home increased the spiral of problems. Her physical strength faltered as the emotional turmoil took its toll. She lost weight, couldn't eat until she was alone and didn't care what she looked like. After all, who was there to see her? She never went out.

Kevin took over the running of the house and meals, leaving her to look after little David. The months passed and intuitively she began to do the right things for her son. He put on weight, gurgled and laughed, lifting her spirits. She was careful to keep the level of noise low, as Kevin would be disturbed. Mother and son bonded strangely as if conspirators against an outer force. No words contributed to this state of affairs, just fleeting expressions and intuitive understanding between Emma and her son. Mother, father and son appeared a normal family to the outside world. Neighbours would compliment Kevin on his little son, now growing into an energetic toddler. He glowed with pride and this rare good mood might last for a day or two if they were lucky. The smallest sign of non conformity to his policy would spark off a tirade of words.

"Slut!" he shouted. "No, more like a lazy slug with trails of slime and dirt around you!"

"All you're interested in is that child," he screamed as she wearily crawled out of bed to calm down the baby.

"When are you going to put me first, call yourself a woman? Who would want you?"

Sometimes, Kevin was so beyond himself, he would wildly throw an offending dish or article across the room. It didn't matter if it hit anyone. More than once she was taken by a penitent Kevin to the accident department at the local hospital. He had pushed her down the stairs in a massive temper outburst and the fall had cracked three ribs. She managed to give a convincing account of how it had happened though the records were there for her own doctor to read. A broken wrist was harder to explain and the pain and nuisance of her arm in plaster more problematic. At regular intervals the same words of justification would spew from his mouth.

"Oh babe, I never meant to do this," he would whine.

"Why do you make me do this? You know how to wind me up, can't you see?"

"It won't happen again, I promise!" he would emphatically state believing it to be true.

The subject of Australia couldn't be discussed after one drastic quarrel between them. Emma had calculated the best time to share her news with Kev very carefully.

"I had a talk with Dad today. Don't worry it was on his phone bill," she quickly added.

"He wants to pay for a holiday for us so that you can see if you might sometime want to live in Australia." The words hung like a black cloud.

"I can't take the time off!" a sharp reply was flung back.

"No, but you do have two weeks holiday due, don't you?" her timid voice quaked in the air.

"I've got plans for that, why do you always spoil my surprises?" he accused swinging round to face her.

"Kev, it would be a trip you'd love, I'm sure! Don't say no, think about it. Just imagine the flight, the sun, new places to explore," her voice petered out as she saw the familiar signs of trouble in his eyes.

"Shut up, shut up, you're always going on about your family, what about me?" he confronted her edging towards where she stood. Emma's remaining ecstatic feelings that her father had opened up within her trickled down the drain. She had clung on to the hope that Kev would want to show off his son, even if it was only for two weeks.

He jerked her face up from her bowed head and spat out,

"I've no intention of ever going to see your parents or that poxy country."

She was reeling from that final verbal blow, searching for words that might open a future, when he added the ultimate bomb shell.

"Not only am I not going," he ranted, "but more than that, neither is your precious son. I'll make sure you can never take him out of his home and country without my permission. You're going to have to choose, your real family, or your perfect parents!"

The ultimatum, spoken so hatefully reduced Emma to tears. No amount of shouting or threatening from

Kevin could stem the flow. David clung to her desperately, not understanding; his small face puzzled. Kevin bombarded her with flowers later that day, but to no avail, her hope had been blown away. It was many days later that some reconciliation was attempted and a truce called.

Before the summer was over she was pregnant again. Emma made weak excuses to her parents that her health was poor and that she had to delay the thoughts of a visit. She couldn't worry what they made of her refusal, all her energy was needed to restore some peace for David and the new baby. Kevin's tyranny increased and she blamed herself that she caused his anger to flare up so readily. She searched for ways to avoid winding him up, anxiously agreeing to all the new orders he gave. Gradually her outings from the house grew further and further apart. She daren't consider a playgroup or nursery for little David. Kevin had said money was short and, as he held the purse strings, she couldn't disagree. One wage coming in was regularly pointed out to her. Kevin's random inspections increased and he even monitored what his son was doing.

The blows lessened in the nine months of carrying Tina, their daughter. The delivery was normal and Emma was expert at following the tuition she was given. She gained precious minutes from her timed schedule, by slowing down, to show Kevin that his expectations were too demanding. This only opened the door for another slanging match, calling her a slovenly bitch. She had developed a technique of appearing alert to his ravings whilst separating herself from their impact. He didn't recognise how impervious she was becoming to the tyranny of their marriage. Her life, taken under Kevin's control, was unbearable but the two children became her whole world. She cared for and looked after them, taught them to be quiet when their dad was around, and waited. She didn't know exactly what she was waiting for, but it was all she could do.

David's school attendance proved to be her salvation. It opened up a degree of freedom as she delivered and collected him each school day, which Kevin could not interfere with or sabotage. Feeling much stronger now, the new vista of her future helped her to become more assertive. She selected carefully which battles to fight with Kevin, what mattered most to her and the children. Her courage at taking the abuse from Kevin was not known by anyone nor did she admit to it herself.

That morning as Emma sat trembling beside Susie with Tina on her lap, the bubble had burst. Ghostly white, Emma clung to her friend. The others in the group diplomatically drifted away in twos and threes to leave Susie alone with her. Incoherently, she blurted out that David, now at school, was safe for the moment. She had to get him away. The words were painful and drained away the last shreds of self control. Between lengthy bouts of sobbing and the search for words to explain her family life, Susie comforted the thin body of Emma.

Slowly the full picture emerged of Emma's life and this particular morning. David had annoyed his dad, messing about with his breakfast. Shouting and dragging his son upstairs, Kevin had flung him into his bedroom until it was school time. Banging the front door shut as he left, Kevin didn't care about the turmoil he left behind.

David, crying and begging to be let out, had a huge weal on his back, left by the cupboard door's impact as he fell into the room. Emma comforted her child and restored some degree of normality for the three of them. Her mind racing with millions of thoughts took over from her usual emotional reactions. She had to protect her children but first gain a breathing space. They must leave the house quickly before Kevin returned. Routines of preparing for school took over and she breathed more easily as the little boy, pleased to see his friends went into the safe haven of school.

Trembling, she made her way to the bench with Susie. She had made up her mind.

"I will make a new life for us, I can do this, I can, I will," she convinced herself.

She would never return to her home again as Kevin's wife. He had gone too far this time. The children were not going to suffer under his rule.

The school, doctors, police and her family would all have to be told now. Any shame she felt was unimportant, she had to get the children out of his reach. Subconsciously she had been facing this moment for a long time but never confronted it. At the back of her mind she accepted that the issue of Kevin's paternity would be an obstacle for life. She would never be able to join her parents in Australia.

"One step at a time," she remembered her mother saying "don't worry about tomorrow, deal with today."

Susie, dumbstruck for the first time in a long time eventually resumed some normality. Reassuring Emma, she phoned her husband. Working in the police force had some advantages, though she hadn't thought her husband would be dragged into this predicament! Together, she and Emma would collect David from school immediately and take the first step in the process and go to the police. There were many obstacles to jump, but now there was hope. Emma felt almost euphoric as the head teacher showed her into the office.

The leaves of the sycamore tree rustled about the now empty bench. It seemed it was almost satisfied with the outcome of the drama played underneath it over the last two hours. Ideas of a prosaic leaning would suggest that the wind was increasing, forewarning of the stormy weather to come that day.

Birds, nesting and rearing their young in the branches, would soon be getting ready to migrate for the winter. The time for protection was no longer necessary.

Emma's plight now urged her to turn away from the security of her marriage, as in reality, it had turned to control and captivity. The ivy that clung and bound itself around the roots and bark of the tree, replicated the characteristics of her husband Kevin.

Freedom and independence were worth striving for to survive.

Chapter 5

The itchiness of Dave's skin always reminded him of the luxury of bathing. He missed this regular habit enormously with his chosen lifestyle. Sometimes he treated himself to the price of a session at a swimming pool. He could linger under the showers there, wash and shave without spectators, and then enjoy the pleasure of a swim. He hadn't been able to afford this just recently so he would have to resort to the public toilets. These were becoming scarce in some towns, as the council's reduction in spending had closed down many of them. The shopping malls supplied better conditions to clean up, but these weren't open as early and often he was moved on by cleaners.

Today he was hoping to sort himself out early, so he could get round to the nearby building site. He had heard they were behind schedule for a huge job in the area. He hoped he might be taken on as a labourer to release the permanent staff for more skilled work.

He was in luck, the toilets were open though far from clean from the drunks and party goers of the night before. Dave didn't waste time, he hurried, splashing the cold water on his skin. The soap dispenser was low, but just enough to wash his hands and face. Shaving in cold water often caused cuts, but he needed to look more presentable. He must hurry, it was already gone eight thirty and the building site would be in full swing. It had taken him far too long to get here. The first toilet had been locked so he had made a detour to find this one. The site was a good half hour away even if he jogged. He knew the site foreman wouldn't consider him for work if he smelled or looked like a tramp. It was worth the effort to look more normal.

Finished and gathering up his bag, he left the place and jogged onwards hoping he would be in time.

Chapter 6

12 noon

The hours sped by with the usual procession of determined walkers crossing the park. Occasionally one would stop for a brief moment, checking their bags and purchases. No one seemed to have time to pause or want to use the bench under the sycamore tree. Twelve chimes rang in the air and in no time Romeo and Juliet materialised. The pseudo names used by each other kept them anonymous and were highly appropriate to the actual circumstances of their life. They called each other these selected names, they would never risk their own. The young lovers escaping from their Capulet and Montague schools were careful to disguise their route to the park.

Romeo had raced away from school on his bike, eager to be unnoticed by his class mates. They teased him at how quickly he made his exit from the last study session, unable to get out of him where he went each lunch time. He was a solitary soul and though most people liked him, they could never puncture his detachment. One of the few adolescents that seemed secure and self reliant, he didn't need to accept any of his school mate's demands.

A tradition of enmity between the two local secondary schools had been nurtured with each new year entry. Continuity of the competition and prejudice between schools had grown up. Reason or fairness were unemployed concepts. The two schools and their team of staff had worked to reduce the tension between their pupils and respective counterparts, but had never been able to completely stamp it out. Parent associations and sixth form combined ventures had produced limited success. Transitory small victories had all too soon been swamped by larger serious battles. Occasionally sports events led to an outward show of strength and superiority. Numbers of press ganged students were rounded up to show muscle and nerve.

Sometimes verbal battles spilt over into physical fights which the teachers struggled to control. Often the confrontations were arranged in out of school hours so the schools' input was minimised. Nor should it be supposed that this hostility was confined to the school environment alone. In truth, the neighbourhoods built around the schools harboured the same antagonistic ethos and ill conceived beliefs. Which one, school or surrounding, had spawned the initial belligerence? No one could remember the start of it all, but now a gang like culture patrolled the streets intent on maintaining their own borders and community.

It was imperative to make the residents comply to the rules. The teenagers knew that acceptance of this warring situation was paramount for their own safe school existence. Romeo, however, had more than this gang culture to worry about. He had strong family reasons to keep his lunch time meetings secret.

He was heading for a place rarely used by school mates in the lunch time period. It was too far away to make on foot in the time allowed. The bike gave him extra precious minutes to spend with his one true love. The tree had been discovered by him when seeking out peace, to read undisturbed and not be interrupted for some mindless activity by his friends. Romeo leant his bike against the bark of their tree, out of breath, pleased that Juliet was already there. A quick furtive embrace and kiss, and they bubbled over with chatter and news.

Juliet was lucky that each period before lunch was timetabled for free study. She could make her way unnoticed to their secret place. Her own rival school was largely made up of different ethnic groups and cultures. Rarely did anyone leave the premises for lunch, they were grateful for the schools' attention to diet and the provision made. She tried not to look different and used her parents' strict routine to explain to close friends where she was going. It was unlikely that a comparison would be made of her stories. School friends and family social gatherings rarely mixed.

Romeo and Juliet had agreed that all contact between them was to be here, under the old tree, face to face. Phones, email, Facebook or any other method of communication had unanimously been discarded as points of contact. They were all too well aware that these systems could be intercepted and misused by others. Their peer groups were unknown entities and unpredictable. They didn't want their judgement or the chance of sabotaging their plans.

So, from the very first date, after their meeting in the book shop, they met here or left notes in a crevice in the trunk. Oblivious of earlier sweethearts over the decades, who had used this posting system, they believed in their unique purpose for the tree. Romeo had met Juliet in town, both visiting the extensive bookshop for extra study material. Their hands had brushed each other as they reached for the same revision guide. Laughing at the absurdity of wanting the same book, they had spoken easily of their respective courses at school. Juliet, aware that her mother would catch up soon from her shopping, had cut the dialogue short. She had wanted to stay and talk longer, but it might be unwise to push her limited freedom.

Romeo, a regular customer to this particular book shop, made very sure that for the next few weeks he was around the place. His patience was rewarded when she turned up. A coffee accepted by Juliet gave them more time to talk. The joy of recognising a like minded student oiled their interest, and a new chemical attraction fuelled a future likely date to meet up. Without using words to explain their backgrounds they intuitively knew to keep their own council. The park as their venue, and precise time arrangements were finalised between them. This was to herald regular visits to the park and tree where they shared common interests and talked of their dreams. Amazingly the differences between their home lives interested and intrigued each other. They began to bond with common problems and grew to love how solutions became simple when they discussed them. What seemed to be huge mountains to them individually, became mole hills as a pair. Both learned how to deceive their parents when they remarked on how much happier their child appeared. They covered their tracks of discovery and longed for their special time, however short it was.

The casual friendship became stronger and, when they finally accepted they were in love, the new prospects ahead daunted them. The obstacles in front of them could so easily explode into a feudal conflict involving schools, neighbourhood and certainly their families. Much wiser than their age might indicate, they worried at the problems facing them, and put both their considerable brains to work it out. The resolution to their liaison was painstakingly planned, details and predictable outcomes mulled over, until the final scheme was nearly complete. The couple had to discuss the last items, their voices quiet and engrossed, they were aware the lunchtime was passing too quickly. Time was running out for them. When the exams were completed the plan would be put into action on the day of their results. They must make every second count and check the details of their scheme.

Neither of them wanted to follow Shakespeare's story line for his lovers. The parallels to their own position became all too clear as they studied and understood, through literature, the dangers of prejudice and ongoing vendettas. They applied themselves to the pitfalls ahead. They would be different, surely a better outcome was waiting for them. They just had to make it happen.

Romeo's childhood had been modern and liberal when his small family reached the UK. The small boy could vaguely remember the strangeness of this country after the rural surroundings of their native land and small village. Readily accepted by the immigrant community in which they settled, his parents added to their own family, Romeo was the eldest of six. Each child was loved and welcomed into the whole family of aunts, uncles, and grandparents. His father had set up a small cafe, and worked ceaselessly to support them all. The enterprise tackled with the exuberant personality of his father attracted customers. Boisterous, infectious singing rang through the kitchen door, wafting alongside the enticing smells of cooking. Laughter echoed around the walls as their troubles and solutions were aired for anyone to hear. Customers were eagerly greeted and welcomed into the simple surroundings, even encouraged by a favourite aria or current tune. His culinary expertise became know in the district and, soon help was needed for the future of the business. Romeo's mother worked alongside her husband when she was able. Numerous pregnancies interrupted the daily hours needed, so kitchen staff were employed from their relatives and community.

Romeo knew how desperate they were becoming as they waited for him to finish his education and join them as a chef. He had watched and been taught the basics of cooking, but in his heart he knew it would give him no real satisfaction or joy. Expansion or success to a chain of restaurants, would only lead eventually to managing other people. He really couldn't see himself pushing people around. Romeo resembled his father, curly hair, brown eyes and a deep love of family life. His mother, a devout church goer, gave him his love of solace, quietness and a depth of the spiritual elements of life. This contrasted with the pair who were a loud, volatile couple with dramatic tendencies to laugh and cry for all to see.

The couple could not account for the differences in their eldest son from their other children. Romeo was thoughtful and calm, a keen reader and introverted character. Once settled into the senior school he loved studying, preferring the company of books to any sport or leisure pursuit. It seemed that none of his brothers or sisters followed in his footsteps. He had an enquiring mind so school work engrossed and motivated him further, resulting in high grades. He was a perfect candidate for university and was predicted an easy road to success in his exams. Romeo's parents humoured his idea of university life and held back from speaking or pushing him to leave at the end of the final year.

They believed that he would accept the need to help his father in the restaurant, he had never let them down in the past. Enrolling for places at the various universities had been swallowed without too much arguing. They would wait and see, sure in the knowledge that their tradition would entice him back into the fold. The biggest obstacle to integrating his love, Juliet, into the family, Romeo believed would be their disparate religions. It was quite usual for him and his mum to discuss and theorise the doctrines of their faith. As he matured, the questions became deeper and harder for his mother to resolve. Romeo could never accept such important issues at face value. His poor mother, at times, became overwhelmed with his insistent rationalisation of concepts she so readily followed. She loved his natural interest in spiritual concepts but often wished he wasn't so demanding.

Deep within himself Romeo knew and felt the essence and peace of a spiritual belief. He and his mother held this in common and she was relieved and pleased to have steered him in some small part. The exclusivity of many religions, to a certainty that they had the only way to live and die, was the sticking point for Romeo. How could one single faith, hold the key for the cultures and history of the world?

He wanted to debate and argue this stupid concept with her, to persuade and open her mind, but it always resulted in tears. His father would intervene and scold him that it wasn't necessary to demoralise and worry his mother so. Romeo concluded that without the education of history, philosophy and world studies he had enjoyed, it might be too progressive for his mother. After all she was a plain, honest women from a modest background. Now he was faced with a personal need for her to accept and understand cultural differences and he was unsure how to expand or change his parents' convictions. He promised himself that he would take every possible opportunity to avoid hurting his family. He would find a way to make them understand.

The school meeting with the head of the sixth form had ended early; Juliet was pleased as it gave her more time to walk to the park for her reunion with Romeo. These precious moments together were like sparkling diamonds in her life. It wasn't that she was unhappy at home, but rather like wriggling out of a protective skin far too tight for her. She was herself, her own person alongside him. He was her confidant, friend, counsellor and challenger. More than that, he was her love.

The school had been so helpful for Juliet in this last year. As an outstanding student they had assumed university life was self-evident for her future. Juliet's secrecy around applying for the varying establishments had been an unexpected surprise.

The challenges of teaching the sixth form students always stretched their abilities. The school prided itself on meeting the needs of all their children, from whatever ethnic or cultural background. Staff meetings were regularly programmed to solve any problems. Religion, ethnic traditions and dietary requests were tackled. They wanted to excel in these matters, and provide an ethos of tolerance to cover the entire school.

The staff met and discussed the best way to answer Juliet's dilemma. She had already celebrated her 18th birthday so was, in law, an adult. They had put themselves in the position of her parents and had tried to persuade her to talk over her future with her family. The teachers had always found her parents very reasonable and informed. Juliet was adamant that she couldn't take the chance, she wanted their help to enrol for universities.

Accepting that their loyalties were with the student, they had helped with the process of applications to her chosen university. Emails and postal communications came to the school address. Any other contact that was needed was set up and arranged under the umbrella of the school. Visits to the universities for interviews were arranged in the school term. Absolutely nothing was sent to Juliet's home address. The school had no doubts that she would achieve top grades, she was a model pupil. It was such a small thing to keep all paperwork passing between Juliet and the university on the school premises, and was their way of rewarding her effort. Juliet had breathed a sigh of relief that everything was in place and when all exams were finally taken she would wait for the day of the results. Her father, particularly would be eager to know his daughter's achievement.

The family of three daughters and parents had arrived twelve years ago when Juliet had been eight years old. Her two younger sisters and parents, reasonably fluent in the English language, had adjusted quickly to their new surroundings. Juliet had been proud of her father. As a doctor he held esteem in the community and the new country they now lived in. More than that, Juliet was grateful that her father's liberal approach to her education was so unlike many of her associates at school. They valued and promoted an ethos of study, seeking to improve and benefit their children. It seemed to Juliet a dichotomy that, while appreciating the schooling in the UK as a means of enlarging horizons, they were restrictive to using the many amenities on offer.

She wore the clothes, jewellery and varying aspects of her culture, particularly in her younger years. But, as she was shown a wider viewpoint of the world, the realisation of the severe regime she endured, began to permeate her mind as to how much she was missing. Concepts of the history and emergence of women in many countries over decades that she learned about at school fascinated her, in her largely male dominated family.

The contrast between differing parts of the world and women's influence on it, interested her so much. She had resolved to look into this in her university studies. At home she had noticed how animated her mother became at similar topics she came across. Her mother never seemed to explore them further. Why didn't she read more about the emancipation of women? Why accept so readily the male viewpoint? Perhaps in her mother's heart she knew this might undermine her happiness and cause conflicts. Her mother was fully aware that domesticity had been her birthright. She lived her life through her daughters, revelling in their enthusiasm and new horizons. She bathed herself in their triumphs and vicariously enjoyed their successes.

Juliet vowed that wouldn't be enough for her, she wanted to make a difference. Within the large extended family a name was whispered, but when she sought out more details the answers were vague or deliberately ignored. Questioning her mother closely in a private moment of time, she found out the answer to the mystery. It was known within the whole family that her third cousin had disgraced her parents by running away. It was muted that she wouldn't agree to the arranged marriage planned for her. By mutual consent her name was never openly heard in conversations. If by chance a mention of her cropped up, furtive glances and lowered comments quickly erased the moment.

Juliet knew that her cousin still lived in the country, she had rescued a letter torn up in her aunt's house. Deviously hiding it in her clothes she had pieced it together. Reading it had answered her curiosity. Unknown to her parents, Juliet still kept the address of her cousin. She admired her courage, though this was not to be spoken of to anyone. One good thing had resulted from her new information, it had set her on a path to find out what records or paperwork were existing on her life. Unable to sleep one night, she had quietly made her way to her father's office and into the desk drawer. Her birth certificate, passport and immigration details were there, neatly kept together. She loathed herself for the deceit, but it quelled the wild speculations that her young mind kept exploring.

The widening gulf that was now appearing between her parents and herself was hated by Juliet. Were they aware of it? She didn't know, but she tried even harder to be the daughter they deserved. It seemed so easy for her sisters. Why did she make such heavy weather of her life? The inner struggle engulfed her and she felt exhausted, fighting the conflict within her. The heavy boulder of her restricted life pressed down on her and she spiralled, descending into the murky waters. Panic rose like gasping bubbles from her mouth. Romeo's appearance had allowed a glimmer of sunshine to flood in. There was no way she wanted her prison to envelope her again. She yearned for the warmth of the possibilities now before her, alongside him. The scales of love were weighed now in his favour.

Juliet dragged her mind back to the present, conscious that the precious minutes of their lunch time were speeding away. Their plan was in place. They had, together, worked out all the possibilities. Consigned to memory only, they drilled each other with the details, they couldn't risk putting anything on paper.

"We both have acceptance places for our chosen universities, has yours come through yet?" he would ask for the umpteenth time.

"The confirmation came some time ago, is that why you forgot it?" she replied.

"Sorry, my love, but we must get in together to the same place or we'll need to rethink our alternatives."

They had to consider their choices carefully. It was decided that Juliet would begin her course the same year in the autumn. Romeo had judged that his study needed to be deferred for one year. This would allow him to use his catering skills to find a job. They needed to conserve any money coming in from student loans and their meagre savings brought with them. Romeo would begin his university course one year later when their debts were kept to a minimum by his earnings.

They had worked on the very tight schedule for the first four weeks. The train boarded on that crucial day of the exam results would take them a substantial distance to a coastal town where they would merge as holiday makers. A cheap B&B had been booked and they would make doubly sure that all the necessary papers were with them. This subterfuge would test their ingenuity beyond anything they had done so far!

Romeo had saved hard for their first weeks away and the cost of their marriage. He had hoarded away any money given to him for birthdays or Christmas. The family knew he was saving for something big but so far unspecified. Money earned working alongside his dad went into the fund. Dad had guessed and casually spoken about helping to pay for driving lessons, but his son had only grunted words that seemed to agree. The sum Romeo had collected ought to pay for the licence and registry office bill. If they were lucky and careful there would be enough for the holiday.

"We can always sell our phones or laptop if we're struggling," he had assured her.

"I've got a little jewellery, but I would like to avoid using that if possible," she had offered.

"There's no need, I can get a job waiting on tables for a week or two. It's a hectic period around holidays for cafes, I don't mind kitchen work even." Romeo calmed down their anxious thoughts at what they were about to do. Contacting the Registry Office on the school computers told them what necessary documents they needed to have ready to book the wedding date! The lovers would marry as soon as possible. The legal union would ensure there was no turning back.

Juliet felt only a few nerves about their scheme, they would use these early days to find out about each other. She had no doubts that they would grow in their love without the furtive snatches of time they had so far experienced. They had calculated that, once they were married, they would move to their university city and find student lodgings. Romeo would set about finding permanent work, only then would they contact their families. They needed to have as many obstacles solved as possible.

Forecasting the reception from their parents was impossible, or how the next three or four years would unfold. The couple hoped that they would be welcomed back into their respective families alongside their new spouse. At what point, and in what time frame, they had no notion. That rested with others. They dreaded the path to reconciliation! An immediate problem was how to secure time and space undetected on that special morning of the escape. Romeo was the first to interrupt their musings.

"The date for our results is the 8th. I've let mum know that I'll phone her with my exact grades. She's expecting I won't be home until the evening. My classmates have planned to hang out together, celebrating or commiserating. So that makes it easy to slip away to meet you at the station. What have you told your parents?"

Juliet had felt uncomfortable when she had stumbled in on a private conversation between her parents. She was sure that they were organising some surprise for her. Her senses more acute than normal, told her it was something big. She wasn't feeling pleasure, rather apprehension.

"I'm really worried," Juliet replied. "My father is so keen to come with me for the results and thank the staff. I've told him I'll be helping to sort out books for next year so that might gain us a couple of hours. I need to get away as quickly as I can though for the train time. It's going to be hard!" Romeo searched her anxious face as she added one more lie to the mountain of dishonesty. If only it didn't have to be this way!

"I've written my goodbye letter to Mum and Dad. I think I might phone them from the train to tell them where to find it," he told her.

"That's not possible for me. I've thought what to write, but I'll do it at school. One of the staff will give it to my father when he arrives to collect me. It should be safer for us, don't you think?" Juliet's miserable eyes spoke volumes to him.

"We can still change our minds, my love. I'll wait for you no matter what happens," Romeo reassured her. Juliet shook her head solemnly.

"No, it's the only way. I can't risk our future. My father is certain he knows what's best for his daughters, I can't take the chance, there's too much to lose!"

Romeo comforted her as she dried her tears, reluctantly leaving her to make his way back to school. More in control of herself, Juliet resolved she had one more job to do at school before the term ended. She would persuade her favourite teacher to try and keep her secret plans for university away from her parents for as long as possible. She was conscious that their information of her plans would eventually have to be shared. Deliberately she had not divulged which of the six universities was her favourite. So the trail for anyone to follow would be full of problems.

"Better still," she mused, "it's going to be even harder as no one will know my new name!" She quickened her pace, leaving the park gate, rehearsing in her mind the letter she must write.

Dear Father & Mother,

I am so sorry for the shock you will get when you read my letter. I don't want to hurt you in any way, for you have given me all your love.

I must go away for a time, I need the space to follow my own life. I hope you can wait for me to call you in a month's time. I will be safe and I promise you I will get in touch.

Forgive me,

Your loving daughter.

A hazy sun shone through the leaves above the bench. The sorry scene below its boughs would have produced much for Shakespeare to ponder over. Lovers' troubles had come and gone through the years under the tree's canopy. Hovering in the air that midday, the silent witness longed for their outcome to be a happy one.

The branches of the tree, shooting off from the main trunk, complemented each other. Growth directed on all sides, with differing shapes, all existing healthily from one source. How opposite to the man made problems of the human race, focusing on their contrasting ethnic backgrounds, religion and traditions.

The hopes of Romeo and Juliet to overcome these trivialities would succeed with their love and, they trusted, with their families.

Chapter 7

He had been too late! Dave had jogged up to the building site, wheezing and rasping in a distressed state. The site resembled a nest of ants each one intent on their part of the whole. No room for him to fit into, the foreman shrugged away his guilty thoughts as he turned Dave away.

"Come earlier next time, mate!" he called over his shoulder. A self-made man, he would have liked to give him a chance. What to do with the morning? Dave's ideas rumbled around his empty head, devoid of the drugs to clear it.

The library would be warm and quiet, a welcome time off his aching legs. An unobtrusive corner of the room was his preferred place, away from the scrutiny and stares of the locals and their disapproving expressions. He could use the free papers to see if there were any likely jobs he might apply for. The computers might be available to hack out some kind of employment record. More than once he had been asked for some paperwork to prove his abilities, so he would need to embroider the facts, without giving away too much of his history.

Dave was not feeling well today, his stomach cramped in pain. These last couple of weeks he had pushed aside ideas of contacting a doctor, preferring to hope he would feel better soon. He had lost weight, some of his clothes now hung on him and he felt continuously tired. Alcohol now was avoided, any money he had was spent on food. The waves of tiredness overpowered him in the warm, quiet atmosphere of the library, and in no time at all he was asleep. A hand jolted him into consciousness as an irate voice reminded him that libraries were not provided for sleeping purposes. Acutely dismayed at the heads turned in his direction, he gathered his few belongings and made an embarrassed exit. An upward glance at the clock confirmed he must now hurry to get to the next place for help.

'The Cornerhouse' a non-denominational charity had survived the recent funding problems and Dave was heading for it. It provided a hot meal daily for the homeless towards which they were expected to contribute something. Dave had saved his last few coins to give himself the nourishment his body so needed. It didn't matter what the meal might be, he would enjoy the luxury today.

Dave had never fully used the many facilities that this charity had on offer though they had been clearly pointed out to him. He could have booked into the use of a bath or shower as he was a regular visitor. Twice a week nurses were there to solve minor aches and pains, or give advice. A doctor was present once every week for a limited two hours, alongside a chiropodist. Foot and leg ailments were common problems from living on the road. Dave kept these in reserve for harder times, he could look after himself, things would look up soon, he promised himself.

Volunteers were around in the weekly schedule to assist in filling out official forms, helping to find work or finding a permanent home. It was the cycle of despair that was the hardest to break into though. No permanent address was a barrier to a job. No employer to act as a reference meant few landlords wanted to let a home to these unreliable, prospective tenants. The struggle daunted the most enthusiastic helper and reinforced the futility for these pathetic nomads. The stories of their separate lives highlighted poor choices, bad luck and inadequate backgrounds which led them to this situation.

Dave's usual stubbornness turned away their offers of help judging that the questions they would ask would be too high a price. The wall built around his privacy issues could not be assaulted. He had accepted a replacement pair of boots from their supplies and had been grateful for the comfort. Today the meal was tasty and substantial, he felt noticeably strengthened. He would stay there until mid afternoon but knew he had to raise some cash quickly.

It was a long time to go without food or drink until this time tomorrow, he would need a warm drink at the very least. Reviewing his options, he reckoned that he must leave now and head for the precinct. If he could use the next three hours before the shops closed he might make enough money to pay for a meal tomorrow and a snack that evening. He would beg and see what happened. His strange ideas allowed him to do this without censure. He could ask strangers for cash, but couldn't take the support on offer around him. The volunteers at the Cornerhouse shook their heads as Dave ambled away. How much longer would it be before they could infiltrate his resistance?

Dave sat down in the corner near the lifts of the shops. He always sat to rest his legs, his head well below eye contact. He copied the traits of the animal world and their subservience to the stronger creatures around them. People didn't like eye contact in his situation, they didn't want confronting with the plight of another human being. If he was too obvious it wasn't long before he was moved on out of the warmth and onto the roadside.

Certain that this was the right place to get any results, he laid out his cap and waited.

Chapter 8

2.00 p.m.

Carefully lowering his seventy eight year old body onto the bench, Keith was relieved that his knees hadn't given out on him during the afternoon stroll. It was true, he admitted to himself, his old frame had a few aches and pains. He was grateful that his active life hadn't caused too much trouble. More than that he realised his brain had become clearer over the last couple of days. He knew for certain what urgently needed to be done. He was ready for the next few days ahead, resolved to make a difference!

Keith undid the bag and pulled out a thermos flask, together with two mugs. He placed them on the flat surface of the seat and poured out the steaming tea.

"Here we go, Janet, this is just what the doctor ordered," he muttered aloud, "I didn't forget the sugar today, it's just as you like it"

Sipping slowly at the hot liquid, he revelled in the knowledge they were together, still enjoying the simple pleasures that was their routine. Abruptly the shock replaced his reverie when he felt the now stone cold tea left untouched by his side. Grasping yet again that Janet was dead, he faced the truth in this never ending nightmare.

"Dad," his daughter Helen had said, "you can't hang onto your old life with Mum. Things have to change a little, but you can remember all the good times".

It didn't matter what they all said, Janet was with him in every part of the house, in all their routines and habits of fifty years. He kept to the pattern, talking with her as he made their meals, attacking the chores and taking her with him on their strolls. He felt the peace of her presence alongside the knot in his gut as he came to terms with reality. Keith's adjustment to bereavement followed its own path, it couldn't be channelled into phases expected by those around him. They had worried when he constantly spoke aloud to her, when he returned to the past, not wanting to consider the future. It was all he could do to survive the day, let alone plan anything. The memories were kinder, softer and soothed the empty place within him.

He had nursed Janet in the last few days of her life, grateful that she could be at home. The frail flesh of his wife he disregarded, as he cared and cherished the light that shone from his young sweetheart's eyes. Married for over fifty years, they were two parts of a whole, full of shared memories, complementing strengths and weaknesses. Keith couldn't cast off her influence, so kept her alive around himself.

"I've been so wrapped up in myself," he muttered to the tree, "Janet, I've let you down, I didn't hear or see what's in front of me. I've got it organised now, you wait and see. Tomorrow will show them, they can't just cut it down!"

Turning round to the tree under which he sat, Keith touched its bark. He traced his initials alongside his dear wife's. Freshly carved letters almost touched the same spot and he wondered if the young man he'd seen earlier had demonstrated his love the same way. Several times he had watched the two young people meet up and talk intensely, so obviously in love. Keith had waited for them to leave, he wouldn't intrude though he recognised the boy. He was certain that the restaurant his grand daughter was so fond of, was where he'd seen him. Sophie was so generous she wanted to include Keith and Janet on special occasions. The young man had served their table efficiently and quietly despite the frenetic atmosphere of the place. The couple, he noticed today, were in a world of their own, oblivious and focussed and he would leave them that way.

Keith drifted back to the day he carved their names. He had, as a young man, rambled over the countryside gulping in the fresh air and admiring the cattle and sheep grazing on the nearby farm. He would stand and watch the farmer busy and preoccupied, always focussed on another task to be done.

Several times, men of his age working in the fields would wave him over the footpath. Sometimes, if he was lucky, he would glimpse a young woman and hear the farmer calling to her for help. It was clear the family members were part of the farm life, working as a team beside their father. Janet had eventually spoken to him, as he became a frequent visitor using the footpath.

"Make sure you close that gate!" she shouted, "we've prize cattle here, don't want them getting out!"

He had quickly slammed it back in place, hoping she didn't think him a complete fool. Before long their chattering, however brief, became eagerly anticipated by both of them, much to the amusement of Janet's brothers.

The teasing and comments of her family went unnoticed by Janet. Her dark curly hair was bent over books, an avid reader, Janet's thoughts were always somewhere else. Wartime education had been limited and a generation of children had suffered short hours and large classes. Children had been filtered out of a grammar school system unless their intelligence test proved them worthy of this method of schooling. Janet as a late developer and product of a secondary school, proved herself to be clever and bright. Though these schools were unfairly recognised by many to be inferior, she had against the odds, become a self educated, perceptive young woman. She grew to like her meetings with Keith, as she recognised a kindred spirit in his beliefs. Keith loved the farm and was soon given work on a full time basis. His aptitude for the land and animals made him a valuable asset. He filled in the holes left by her brothers as one by one they were conscripted to join the reserve army.

"It's a damned nuisance this conscription," Janet's father would grumble, "wouldn't you think they had enough of our young men in the last war?"

Conscription seemed a necessary evil after the World War 11 was over. Every young man over the age of eighteen would have two years spirited away from his life, to march, drill and complete army, navy or air force training. It turned teenagers into men and fashioned them into conforming to a national image for the world to see. Keith would argue with Janet's father over the aftermath left by two consecutive world wars as they went about their mundane jobs.

"What a mess your generation has left us." he would complain, "we're still mopping up the effects, rationing has only just finished and there's still not enough houses for everyone." The reply came fast and direct.

"You don't know you're born lad! Try living through that time, homes blasted, men disabled or not coming back at all, women working in jobs too heavy for them. I don't know what you find so difficult, we're putting it right, just wait and see."

Keith catapulted back into the present, realising that once again he was muttering to the tree. He shook his head, he really must stop doing that. People would think he was losing his mind, he needed to show them he was capable and sane.

"You and I have known each other far too long," he whispered to the tree, "trust me, I won't let it happen." A flame of indignation grew inside him when he thought of the fate of his old friend fanned by his recollections of life with Janet. They had battled against issues they could see were wrong, Janet had loved his fiery personality as he strove to make things better. A regular pattern was forged with the two watching for potential harm to nature and their countryside. Plants, animals, earth and air became their dependants. They were custodians of today and tomorrow. They campaigned within the law but with a fervour that would last throughout their lives.

Janet and he married, living at the farm with her parents. It was easier and cheaper allowing time to work and play. The explosion of pop music and the rock and roll dance craze astonished many as a new era of fun and freedom enveloped Britain. It seemed to cast off the post war gloom and attitudes lightened. Simultaneously some minds grew anxious as nuclear power advancement sped forward at an alarming rate.

"Why can't we see the dangers before us?" Keith demanded of his father in law. "We don't want another war; we don't need nuclear power; it's too costly and a threat."

"You forget very quickly, lad," his father-in-law retorted, "it's only five years ago since we had the great smog of London, do you want that again?"

Keith remembered well enough, as a young lad he had heard about the fatalities that followed. The coal-fuelled smog hung over the city for five days, in a windless, cold, pea souper. The death of 4,000 people, 100,000 illnesses, and a subsequent further 8,000 deaths were attributed to this man-made phenomenon. He knew that there was a pressing need for change to reduce smoke pollution. He watched the new power stations, constructed away from cities, marching over his beautiful landscape. Battling within himself the need for progress weighed against conserving the earth. How did he reconcile nuclear power against the pollution of fossil fuel?

"Janet and I are going on the Aldermaston March, Dad. We both feel it's the right thing to do," he told the family that evening.

The two of them had discussed the nuclear bomb development which seemed to be accelerating. They wanted to add their voices in protest, hoping they could influence events. They didn't care about the party politics some were promoting, but had their eyes fixed on changing the future.

It was then that Keith faced how little he really knew about those powerful, educated opponents. He needed knowledge to validate and confirm his sentiments. Regrets at not pursuing further education when it had been offered to him, confirmed he would make sure his children would get a better chance of a university place. Evening classes would have to be the answer for him though. These provisions supplemented vocational aspects and gave qualifications, whilst holding down a job. Sometimes as apprentices, the company would send them on day release. Once a week the young people would return to college to learn the theory around their work, both parties benefited and improved the quality of their work.

Year after year, Keith joined night classes on environmental subjects, helping him become more proficient in conservation of the resources. He specialised in researching trees and was respected by many. Stroking the rough side of the trunk, Keith's memories of family occasions flooded in. The long walks with Janet ending up under its boughs to kiss a fond farewell. The last goodbye before he left for conscription into the army. They had planned their marriage, finally leaving the farm to rent a small house within sight of their special tree. Years of pleasure from picnics, birthday parties and family gatherings, so many took place in this favourite spot.

The creeping fingers of development around the tree had long since nibbled away, in favour of houses, shops and schools with all the attributes of progress. Snugly in their home in those years Janet had fought her battles over the encroachment onto green belt land. Their protests included the noise pollution from nearby highways as car ownership increased and Britain's wealth touched more people. The country boomed with new industries and car manufacture. Janet researched and gained support from many she met but rarely did they win against these forces. At best they only deferred development to another time or entrepreneur.

The small Morris Minor they now owned chugged Keith and his family along to favourite seaside haunts. Camping holidays allowed them to ramble, climb and pursue so many outside interests. Richard, their first child, was born and Janet still helped out on the farm even though Keith had moved onto forestry work. Nursery places were scarce so the little boy spent his first years exploring the farm, toddling by his Grandpa.

All around the young couple the pulsing sixties throbbed with the music of the new stars, the Beatles.

Music liberated the scene, together with mini-skirts and knee length boots. London became the centre for fashion and cutting edge trends. Sexual freedom for women accelerated as usage of the new birth control pill became free and common practice. No longer were random pregnancies necessary. Equality and unfettered prospects were attainable for any woman. However, the promiscuity that the pill allowed was to be the catalyst that influenced and alarmed many. Subsequent generations inherited the changing attitudes of the time. In the span of his lifetime Keith was amazed at the changes that rained down. He considered the aftermath of the Second World War, the so called 'Cold War' between Russia and the West. Several national wars followed in Korea, Vietnam, Yugoslavia, and the Middle East which sucked other nations into their conflict.

The eruption of development in space technology, leading to the first man to stand on the moon, excited and enthralled Keith. Satellite expansion followed which led to the growth of phone links and the advancement of mobile phones. Keith remembered how Richard as a young lad had watched Star Trek on television and been so excited at the hand held communicators Captain Kirk had used. Who could have guessed this imaginary idea was to be surpassed by real life. Land, sea and air continued to be further explored and challenged by the innovators in Keith's lifetime. Acts of heroism conquered Everest, rowed across oceans, sailed around the world non stop with great feats of endurance.

Keith thought fondly of the personalities of ordinary men and their achievements, Nelson Mandela, Martin

Luther King, people who had made a difference against massive odds. There were so many he wanted to emulate in his small way. In the distance he could hear the ring tones of numerous mobile phones of this new generation. Today's expansion in new technology for computers, phones and electronic communication had opened up the world. People were as near or far from each other as they chose, there seemed to be no limitations in reaching each other.

Keith knew he lagged behind in the skills of computer usage and resolved to bring himself up to date. The grandchildren were only too happy to help. Their faces flew into his mind, spinning him backward again into the past, to his family life. Their daughter, Helen, completed the foursome for Keith and Janet, and the following years sped by in a whirl of work and family nights. Details were blurred in Keith's mind, but he could clearly remember the words of Janet about their children.

"It's a better way, I'm sure comprehensive schools will give parity across Britain," she had explained. She had read the information of its introduction and listened intently to the political and educational propositions. The onerous testing of eleven year old children was to be scrapped. All children would have improved opportunities through this method of education. The aim was to see many more achieving higher standards and reaching the goal of university or college life. Richard and Helen were to be amongst the first pupils to try out the new innovation, tested in America and emulated by Britain.

"Change, change, change, that's all some people want to do," Keith mumbled as he remembered Janet relishing the hopes for their children. "Sometimes it's not as great as it's cracked up to be. We never seem to leave the schools alone. Let them get on with it, do their job."

It had been a surprising stumbling block between the two, rarely had they found themselves in opposing corners. As they felt strongly over this issue it was seldom discussed and they waited for events to prove their own case. Instead they aimed to give their children an appreciation of the land, to show them what was on their doorstep. The little unit scoured the compass points of Britain, absorbing the beauty of a variety of landscapes.

"Mum, why does Dad get so upset and cross?" Richard once asked his mother.

"He's not cross at us, silly, he just wants to help the foxes," his sister would cut in, "I don't blame him, I hate the noise of those hounds chasing them."

Janet would patiently explain the issues around fox hunting and why their dad was so vehement in his reactions. It was still a puzzle to them that their gentle father could show such anger. Richard especially loved the outdoor life together and it was no surprise that he chose to leave school as soon as possible. If Janet was disappointed, she didn't show it but supported his decision. Richard found work labouring at a construction site, absorbing the outside environment. His dreams of following in his grandpa's footsteps were swept aside as the farm was unexpectedly sold. Bovine T.B. had returned to Britain and wiped out the cattle on the farm.

The smell of the burning carcasses and funeral pyres clung in Richard's nostrils even now. Devastated at the loss of his prize herd of cattle, the old farmer had lost all drive to rebuild the farm. Pride in his life's work couldn't motivate him any longer. What was the use? They sold quickly, at a poor price, and found a cottage with a plot of land that they could potter in.

Keith remembered them fondly and grieved at the way their life had ended. He struggled even now with the idea of culling badgers to contain the disease, though it might have helped his father-in law. His love of animals clashed against such a relentless, permanent solution. He was even sorrier that his son couldn't experience farming within Janet's family. Richard was doing well now, Keith reflected. He had worked hard, watched and saved for his chance to set up on his own. Now he ran a company that was well thought of locally. In fact they were now working on a site on the outskirts of his home town. Better still, Richard's two sons were a source of joy that Keith could never have envisaged.

"Oh Janet," he groaned, "how the kids are missing you. They still need you, how am I going to fill your place?"

The image of his son and daughter flew into his mind and of Janet's pride at hearing Helen's exam results. It vindicated all Janet's hopes in the new era of comprehensive education. When Helen graduated at university with an excellent degree, Keith watched the glow on his wife's face.

The career of Helen in meteorology seemed to totally swallow her up. It was a serious job demanding commitment beyond ordinary hours which she loved to give. In the early days of her marriage she balanced time and energy with apparent ease. However, the birth of two daughters had stretched her in a way not fully anticipated. Janet and he had analysed what education had opened up for this generation. It seemed that the emancipation of women, freedom of choice and growing equality had a high cost. A new drudgery was emerging from this progress. A stark contrast could be made between working class women of the Victorian age. Forced to work long hours to provide for huge families was the normal fate for them, they were slaves to the needs of their time and the role in society. What would any of them have thought in this day and age? How could they have believed that modern women actually chose to live their manic hectic life?

Helen's career choice and family life were often in conflict for her effort and time. She juggled with the constraints of each, whilst enjoying the multi dimensional elements of her life. It had become usual for both parents to share in rearing the children, and Helen's husband, Barry, was no exception.

Historically male traits that in the past had lain dormant, became increasingly used and competent, benefiting the families. They were a happy balanced quartet. It was the imbalance of school hours against a working day that proved the most difficult for Helen. Long school holidays and any illnesses were additional problems. Though nursery provision and school clubs filled in some gaps, they could not compete with a loving mother to soothe a child's cries. It was in these circumstances that Helen felt her heart's tug of war. It seemed that the millions of demands for her time made her feel a failure. Everyone expected, in these modern times, that mothers should balance a home, a family, and a career.

"I can't bear to see how tired Helen looks," Janet had confided to her husband, "I must try and help. What do you think?"

Keith and Janet talked it over and offered Helen a solution. Years later, Keith admitted that it was the best thing they could have done. Helen and Janet worked out a schedule for caring for the little girls, supplementing the parents' roles. They filled in the gaps around school and home, enjoying and getting to know Sophie and Kate. Janet became absorbed in her grandchildrens' hobbies and interests. It rejuvenated them and, though often exhausted, they wouldn't have traded their roles for a peaceful retirement. Time seemed to be sucked up and reinvented, playing and finding new ways to please and challenge the girls. In their company days flashed by leaving them like limp balloons,

"Oh Sophie, I know how you miss your gran," Keith brought to mind the closeness of the two.

Sophie, the eldest grand daughter, had become a replica of Janet as a girl. Alert and bright she had inherited her gran's love of books. She dreamed and deliberated quietly, sharing her deep thoughts with only those she trusted. Janet had held Sophie's secret in trust for her. The two had talked and whispered over the question for many hours. Sophie's worries and tears were mopped up by a loving gran in complete privacy. Janet hadn't even shared it with Keith, though he knew she wanted to ask his advice. She waited for Sophie to reach her own decision. The wisdom of hindsight revealed that problems were generally the challenges and turning points that gave the most positive outcomes. Keith accepted that Sophie's early marriage, and beautiful babies had turned out well and he was now a great-granddad.

He was grateful that Janet had been alive to cherish the new baby. Their years had been healthy, though age was insisting on making its presence known. They could feel the nudging of creaking joints, and aching bones as they pushed themselves to remain fit. Medical services were seldom used and they were so grateful for that. Keith was aware of the growing burden that the National Health Service was struggling against, the numerous demands put upon it. It seemed like yesterday that Keith could remember his parents triumphantly praising the new initiatives for free health care in Britain.

Aneurin Bevan introduced the scheme in 1946 after the desperate war demands. The whole country applauded its aims for free health services from birth to grave. It removed the fears that ill health brought, alongside the worries of treatment costs, and lifted the spirit of optimism for the future. Janet and he were so lucky they hadn't used the hospitals much, and when they did the treatment was more than adequate, despite the dire warnings of current thinking.

He wasn't prepared for her illness when it struck, it swept her off her feet overnight. The heavy cold turned rapidly into a feverish bout of influenza that Janet battled against. He ran up and down stairs taking drinks and painkillers, but she grew steadily worse. He called the doctor anxious to get professional help, but the doctor assured Keith that he was doing the right things, time would resolve her high temperature and she would soon feel better. The family popped in and Helen stayed the first night, helping Keith to prepare light food and allowing him to take a rest.

"Go home and get some time for yourself," Keith reassured his daughter. Janet was so much quieter he could easily manage what was needed for both of them. That night he had drifted off into a deep sleep, after making sure Janet was comfortable. Wakening with a jolt from a vivid dream, he felt for her in the stillness. The coldness of her inert body beside him sent waves of disbelief and a heavy weight crushed down on him.

The following hours, days and weeks blurred into one, in Keith's mind. He didn't want to revisit and refresh those dark days. Emotions had drowned any details and he was so grateful that the children had taken over. Janet was as fresh and vibrant as she had ever been in his head. Little wonder that he wanted to talk and include her in his daily tasks.

"I ought to be on my way, I've still got those phone calls to do," Keith disturbed his reminiscences and began to pack up the thermos and cups. He had thrown himself into action the last few days, realising that time was of the essence. Discovering that the tree was imminently to be felled, had appalled him. How could anyone do that? The tree was over a hundred years old, surely it had a conservation order on it? Councils couldn't do that without consultation, or notice of intent. He had to take time to consider and confirm that all the correct channels had been processed by the council and there had been no omissions in the process. The thought that it was his own ignorance and tardiness to react had been a bitter pill to swallow. He was putting it right now, he satisfied himself. He wouldn't let Janet or the tree out of his focus again. Keith faced the reality that he couldn't pursue collecting petitions or canvassing from the local community. He hadn't enough time left for any major push to save this tree. It had to be something immediate, dramatic, a direct action that might ignite surprise or reaction in people. Recently he had felt obsolete and irrelevant to the fast pace around him. He needed to prove to himself and Janet that he could be that pebble thrown into the pond. Who knew where his ripples would end?

On consideration he would use his age to some advantage now. How could anyone ignore a rising eighty year old chaining himself to a tree? He must be a credible, serious advocate for this mission. He didn't want anyone dismissing him as a senile pensioner. He would stop his mutterings, they didn't like it and it raised questions in their minds. Janet was with him, she knew what he was doing. Keith with all his usual thoroughness, had contacted several important dignitaries and professionals. His local MP was well known to the couple, they had campaigned alongside each other several times. He assured Keith he would be there early before he started his day's work. Several journalists were interested in what might be a juicy story. The regional TV company had proved more wary but, when he dropped a few pertinent well-known names they were ready to cover it. He knew that both Richard and Helen had rounded up the kids to help, relieved that Keith was more like his old self.

They were now organising friends and local groups to show their faces on the impending morning. This was familiar ground for him, numbers of people always frightened any opponents.

"We need public support and we can still get it, Janet, just you watch us!"

Keith quickened his pace urging himself to get home, to make sure the troops were marshalled.

Alone again, the bench empty, silence hung around the tree. The warmth of the afternoon was adding to the scorching heat of the last week. Everywhere was parched, waiting for the refreshing rain. Old and gnarled, the root system of the tree was well equipped to survive droughts. It could resist the changes of the elements far better than Keith in his lifetime.

Though Keith had gained pleasure and enjoyed using the tree, he had never copied its ability to bend with events. He confronted change, argued against forces pitched against him or his beliefs.

The compliance of nature with the cycle of life and death, was a contradiction that Keith had yet to accept, however much he had absorbed and loved the countryside.

Chapter 9

Dave emptied his cap into his pocket, the change jingled as he made his way into the churchyard. He had been hustled out of the mall, by an unsympathetic cleaner. The shopping mall hadn't been very busy even though the outside stormy weather often enticed people into the air conditioned surroundings. Dave had sat for nearly an hour before anyone stopped to throw a sprinkling of loose change into his cap. It was laughable to see the lengths some people would go to avoid passing him; unplanned detours around his position, the sudden interest in fumbling into bags, spontaneous interest quickly whipped up to view a showcase window. It was common place to see mothers pulling hesitant toddlers away curious to stare at this strange man.

'Did he worry or threaten their existence?' Dave often thought. Perhaps it was more the anxiety that unforeseen circumstances might change their future events. Could this be their fate if they weren't careful? It was uncomfortable to have their conscience pricked, to have to think about his problems. In fact some people displayed real anger that he had punctured their cosy bubble. Appreciation at any coin given was rewarded by Dave's warm and genuine smile which more than compensated the giver.

"Move on you lazy devil. Can't you see I've work to do? This place is always a mess when you lot hang around," the cleaner thumped his cart to a halt as he spat out the words. "I need to finish this part before I start on the next floor. Find somewhere else to do your begging or I'll call the manager."

Dave scrambled to collect his belongings, thrusting the cap with its contents into his pocket. he didn't want trouble. Sooner than anticipated he found himself outside again in the sticky, still air. It was far too early to return to the park, he would just have to use up the time until dusk. He considered his options as he trailed away from the shops. He really needed somewhere to sit, count up his cash and take stock of himself and his growing urgency to see a doctor. The squat he had found would be occupied by somebody by now. It was ideal for a short stay but obvious to other homeless victims. Aware that thieving was rife, he didn't want to attract attention by counting his stock of money or belongings in front of anyone. Alcohol and spirits would be another potential hazard that would entice him in the safety of closed doors. Mates were always willing to share, acutely aware of the desperate needs of others like themselves. Dave couldn't take the chance knowing his feeble efforts to refuse. He conjured up the sensation of that rich warming liquid trickling down his throat. The welcome euphoria as it did its work, dampening and wrapping his emotions in a blanket. The compulsion of these ideas was difficult to ban from his head. He knew it would take only a split second to revert to his old habits.

Dave dragged his sore tired feet, wincing with the pain. Army training had instilled the need to care for his feet, but of late he had neglected to bother. He had taken the first step towards asking for help by booking in to see the doctor at the Cornerhouse the following day. The workers hid their surprise at his unexpected request but they made no comments.

The retail units were well behind him when Dave passed by a church and graveyard. Struggling with his fiery feet and familiar gut pains he made his way around the back and folded down onto the stones. It was cold and a relief in contrast to the steaming blocks of the streets cowering under the sunlight. The coolness and serenity of the place anointed his agitated spirit. The air around him seemed fresher and soothing. After half an hour he recovered enough to sort out his coat and bag after the hasty exit from the mall. His begging had not brought in much money, there was enough for a meal tomorrow and maybe a hot drink at supper. He would have to do without food tonight, unless he could forage for leftovers around the cafes on route to the park. Sometimes they were rich in pickings, almost a feast if he was lucky.

Dave had found an undisturbed place in the graveyard where few ventured. Overgrown with ivy and weeds he couldn't be seen easily as he fell into a light sleep. Dreams and plans forged together, not readily distinguishable in his mind. Nan's voice wandered in and out together with his mothers, but the voice that insistently broke through was that of his father.

"Dave, you only have one body, one life, it's up to you to look after it. Your body is the vehicle for a future. Treat it badly and you'll never have any choices for your dreams."

He wished now he had fully understood those words, but a teenager throws out such inspirational remarks from a father. Nan's face, worried and troubled appeared entreating him to get help. He sat up and stared around him in a daze. He was alone, just stone gravestones and the dead his only companions. A niggling worm of an idea wriggled into view. The mist swirled in his head, drifting away to expose a clear thought. He would admit to the doctor tomorrow what was really going on in his body and mind. He needed help, he wanted to feel alive again not just existing, able to tackle anything. The zest for life he felt with his army buddies no longer hurt him, in fact it was beckoning him forward.

He would rest here a little more before making his way to the park. Tomorrow would be different, a new start. He held onto this spark of hope.

Chapter 10

5.00 p.m.

Melanie placed her violin case alongside her on the bench, the tree branches gently fanning her face in the oppressive air. The lesson had gone well, but this new piece of music was a challenge. She closed her eyes and could see the mathematical pattern of the bars dance before her. It was always like this, the precise designs of notes formed a mathematical shape. Numbers and repetitions joined together, with the rhythmic pulse of the piece and made sense to her in this foreign world. It was a habit for Melanie to stop in the park and think about her tuition, letting the notes rise and fall in her brain in a comforting way. Melanie struggled with people, school and life in general. She always had, though her mum was the one exception in her insular life. Fifteen years of age hadn't resulted in any firm links between friends and herself. She didn't miss anything, it puzzled her that her mother placed so much importance on friendship.

As far back as she could remember, Melanie recalled those 'chats' that mum gave her periodically, in quiet, calm settings. It had been explained to her that she was a special baby. An infant with needs and gifts that her mum wanted to help her understand. Music had always infused her home, surrounding her and the air she breathed. It calmed her and brought order to her small frustrated body as she grew from infancy to childhood. The tiny form had wailed and thrashed in her cot as her desperate mother fought to understand and contain these sudden outbursts. In the back room through closed doors, the sounds of Alex practicing his violin pieces had entered her young life and brought some sort of serenity to the family. Melanie could vaguely remember his anger when she disturbed his order and focus on the music. It seemed to her that most musicians put themselves first. Her mother had explained how Daddy was busy to the confused toddler and, perhaps to herself, the reason for their poor state of marriage.

Melanie's father was rarely around or in contact. It didn't worry or intrude on the young girl, she didn't look for, or want anything from him. There was no hurt, only a faint realisation that other people lived with their fathers. The constraints of a musician within an orchestra on tour meant frequent and long periods of time away from home. Sarah and he had been compatible as newly weds. She was a natural homemaker, anxious to give the best background to his talent. She cooked and made their nest to suit his needs, ready to make him the centre, eager to praise, love and build his confidence. When he was away she counted the days and waited patiently, unaware at that stage that he craved constant attention and sought it elsewhere. The news to him of their expected child should have been a warning to Sarah as she happily told Alex the dates and showed him the scan.

"It won't fit in very well with my tour, dear," he had moaned. "are you sure we want a child so soon?" It was unthinkable to her that they didn't!

Realising that Sarah's upset was deep and immovable, he reconciled himself to the facts. Perhaps having a child might be good and he consoled himself that as it would make Sarah happy and keep her company when he was away, he wouldn't feel quite so guilty.

He wasn't prepared for his wife's whole time to be consumed by this little person though. His daughter's presence took over their regime and he felt threatened and disappointed. It pleased him that his music played some part in restoring order, but the tiny girl only wriggled and squirmed to be out of his arms when he tried to pick her up. He couldn't placate or calm her down and he didn't like this feeling of failure.

Sarah grew more and more protective of the child and both Alex and she were relieved when it was time for him to return to his schedule of touring Europe. The pattern of family life deteriorated inch by inch and the marriage limped along. Sarah became aware of other women in her husband's life, but knew she couldn't counter the loneliness of the miles between them. Nor could she compete with the admiration and praise of his world of artistic contemporaries in the orchestra.

They were a self-forged unit that knew and lived together in harmony or discord. Each time Alex returned home he would find his little daughter developed more physically but more disturbingly for him, in her strange ways. Melanie was quieter more at peace, but often trance like as she waved and beat her toys to the throb of the music around her. Sarah always had some kind of music playing, though Alex disapproved of some of her taste and choices. It was apparent that the child responded correspondingly to the sounds. Soon, tiny play instruments were preferred to dolls or cuddly toys. In an unexpected show of generosity one day, Alex let her tiny fingers pluck at his precious violin. The temper tantrum that blew up when he tried to take it away alarmed him further.

"That child needs to be looked at, she isn't normal, Sarah. Do something about it, get help"

Alex organised an early return to his work, pleased to pass over the responsibility and to hurry to the safe haven of his new lover. Sarah, restoring calm once again, resolved to answer questions that were forming in her own mind.

"Why did her daughter shrink from the touch of anyone?"

"Was it normal to sit for hours under tables or her cot?"

"Why was it that Melanie was so slow in speaking, though she understood so readily?"

Sarah had nudged these thoughts aside for too long, countering problems with practical solutions, to prove that her lovely child was like everyone else. Her doctor sympathetic to Sarah's worries, suggested that play groups might help to get Melanie to play and meet other children to copy. Melanie would sit on the floor, distant from the pandemonium around her. If anyone touched or entered her space she shrank away and retreated further within herself. The musical games and songs became a lifeline to entice her into the world of make believe. Slowly her social skills grew but could so easily fall apart at any time or from any action by those around her.

Sarah could still remember the shocked look in the eyes of a complete stranger, one day, as he bent over her daughter. She had only left her for a minute at the playgroup, when she heard Melanie's screams and dashed outside to find her head covered in blood where she had banged it. It was deliberate but how could she begin to explain in a minute what would take her a lifetime to understand. Normal children didn't react to a toy snatched away to this degree but Melanie would never be part of that world. Referrals to paediatricians, psychiatrists and numerous professionals were to follow over the months and years. Melanie grew to expect eyes searching and probing her every move. Sometimes puzzles and games stimulated these boring appointments, especially when numbers and shapes were included. She romped through their exercises and tests, excelling and taxing their ingenuity to provide better ones.

It seemed to Sarah that each answer the professionals gave led to more questions until, by the time Melanie had entered the junior school, her mother had accepted there was no definitive diagnosis. The spectrum of Asberger Syndrome was explained and the range of gifts and problems that might, in the future, cause concern. However Sarah had found her own way to keep her child happy, necessity had prompted her search.

Tiny percussion bells and xylophones rang out with small giggles of delight from Melanie. Wooden recorders and harmonicas intrigued and kept the little girl busy in her own world. Sarah bought any instrument that she felt Melanie might handle, none went unwanted in their home. A toy guitar strummed out regularly until, on an unannounced visit home, Alex produced a miniature violin and bow.

Father and daughter had found the bond that linked them together. Alex showed her how to make the sounds as he demonstrated them himself. He couldn't touch or place her fingers to help but contact was superfluous anyway. Melanie, as a sponge, absorbed all she could imitating her daddy in every detail.

Sarah would marvel that the two of them, engrossed in this mutual love of making music, could spend so much time together. Alex never showed much interest in any other part of his daughter's welfare but she was grateful that this link had been found. Every visit home Melanie waited for her daddy to teach her more tunes. She began the rudiments of music theory long before reading skills were tackled. Letters and words could not compete in attracting her attention, her untapped mind could not see their worth.

Alex, for his part, with great patience in these sessions, began to nourish a secret pride in his daughter. She was different, special, in a way that he could understand. It didn't matter about the ability to live with others, he didn't see or want to hear about any problems. No, Melanie's talent he could relate to and boast about to his colleagues. He could bask in her reflected glory, proud of his progeny.

The pattern of the marriage solidified into roles for mother and father. Alex provided the stimulus for music in Melanie's young years, supplemented by a music teacher, chosen and approved of by himself. Meanwhile, Sarah alone, shouldered all the worries and problems. Engrossed with providing stability around Melanie, and supporting her weaknesses, she dreaded the school years ahead. Running the home, together with the numerous appointments surrounding her child's condition, succeeded in absorbing her time and she didn't miss Alex. His visits home became less and less over the years. However, Melanie's meteoritic skills in playing the violin had begun to amaze and threaten her father's confidence and role. Arguments and tantrums from Melanie blew up when Daddy tried to interfere or impose methods upon her. She couldn't be moulded into a carbon copy of himself, or follow all the rules of music.

His patience was stretched and limited. The storms between them would pass and he would gratefully leave. Since he rarely apologised for any of his actions, it didn't occur to him that Melanie might be encouraged to repair the scenes between them. Social norms could not be copied from her daddy.

Sarah was so thankful that Melanie's entrance to school life was not as bad as she had anticipated. Her outings to play groups had paved the way for a calmer introduction to schooling. An uneasy truce was in place between her classmates and herself. They quickly learnt that touching or closeness would lead to hysterics.

Melanie would play, sing and dance with them, but only on her own terms. Fascination at her obsession with numbers, puzzles and music drew them nearer to watch and then ignore her. So the small girl passed through her early years at school learning to tolerate the antics of her age group. Teachers helped her and were challenged to find a syllabus that fitted her needs. Motivating her to work in a variety of subjects was very difficult, sometimes impossible, though she far outstripped the grades in maths. and music. Mainstream maths. Melanie raced through, and so the school resorted to introducing the senior curriculum, to keep her interest and solve disruptive behaviour.

By chance one of the staff, a competent musician herself, was prepared to teach music notation to a small group of children who showed interest. The perfect niche for Melanie who lapped up this extra element to her passion. She began to compose simple and then increasingly complex melodies, taking over spare tedious lessons when teachers were busy elsewhere. Notebooks of her efforts were filled and the pile of them grew and were hidden away.

Meanwhile home conditions worsened as Alex had decided he needed his freedom from Sarah and especially his daughter. His interest and patience with Melanie was exhausted, her demands upon his music were compromising his career. He couldn't possibly fulfil her constant craving for all he knew, she intruded upon his thoughts long after he left the house. She swallowed up his time and left him limp and empty as she sucked him dry. He faced the truth, his daughter was brilliant. She was exceptional, and certainly better than he could ever aspire to be. The strains of the violin concerto escaping from her bedroom touched his heart as never before. The maggot of jealousy grew even fatter each time he came home as he coveted her talent.

Divorce from Sarah was completed before Melanie had reached eleven. His wife baffled by the need to take separation further, accepted that she was losing nothing. Sarah's warmth and love towards him had withered and died. The outpouring of her loving nature had transferred to her child when no love flowed back to restore her aching heart. Any emotional support from him was unthinkable, and they had already agreed a financial package, so really nothing was changed. Occasional visits on birthdays and cards at Christmas would suffice between the trio.

Gradually time increased for Sarah as Melanie could spend more and more time away at school and her music. Sarah, in those first years had been drawn into the web of alternative therapies through her daughter's problems and her circle of friends grew.

The connections between other people struggling to find solutions for their children, formed alliances which were to last longer than ever imagined. Sarah had shared her thoughts on music as a means for therapy with other parents.

"If you want to stop the awful tantrums I believe I've found a way that works for Melanie," she suggested.

"I'd be thankful for any ideas, Sarah, we're at our wits end to cope with Jimmy's energy!"

Any scepticism they may have initially felt was quickly dispelled by the results. Casual small groups were invited to Sarah's home, to share an hour or two under the influence of carefully selected music. The pleasure of this time and comfort together for each parent was vastly outweighed by the effects upon their children. Frenetic, hyper active bodies could be persuaded to use their energy in non violent explosive ways. Tuned to the strains of the melodies, they calmed as the sounds reached an inner depth within. It coordinated random movements, gave expression to their emotions and began to improve communication to those on their outside world. Amateurs at dealing with the various peculiarities of their child, they had hope at last.

Sarah wasn't alone in pursuing any avenue to help her child. Several parents began to pass around likely outlets to follow for help, certain in their mind that knowledge gives power. Sarah had studied music herself and had met Alex at the college where they graduated in the same year. Aware that he was gifted, she had willingly put her own career aside to assist and stay by his side. Now she volunteered at a nearby clinic where they used music as a tool, taking Melanie along. She became invaluable to the staff, realising that adults and children alike could benefit from this kind of music therapy. All spectrums of disabilities could be helped from schizophrenia, cerebral palsy, dementia to physical problems. She had previously no idea of the benefits that music could reach, but realised that it was something she wanted to be involved in. It wasn't long before she enrolled in a college where she could qualify as a registered healthcare professional.

This time happily coincided with Melanie's improvement in accepting small parcels of time, outside of school hours, away from her mother. A carefully selected number of adults were chosen who were willing to focus on creating the right atmosphere for Melanie. The strange girl was no trouble, especially if they allowed her to play her violin away from interference or censure. The lucky venues were treated to mini concerts of Mozart through closed doors unsolicited but a taste of the future. Stranger to all who knew Melanie, was an event which happened one day. She was found chatting easily to an old man living close to her friend's house. Completely unknown to her he had waited for her by his gate and introduced himself. The shy girl was ready to dash away to catch up with her gaggle of friends and parents walking home, when she spied what he was holding, a replica of the case she was carrying.

It was some way along the road before anyone realised they had left her behind. Melanie stood eyes transfixed as the violin case was opened up before her and she saw the most beautiful violin nestled inside. The man quickly explained to the suspicious women retracing their steps, that he wanted to meet up with the girl's mother, if that was possible, for something that might benefit both of them.

Cautiously, the group drifted away, having secured the relevant phone number and address to pass onto Sarah. Sometime later Sarah had met up with him rather reluctantly, first ensuring that the risk was minimised by choosing a local coffee bar for their introduction.

She could hardly believe her ears when he offered to give Melanie the full size violin. Further investigation revealed no hidden agenda or strings attached to the gift. He explained that he had played the instrument most of his lifetime. Now he wanted to pass on the joy to a young musician of the future. The melodies of Mozart, Bach and Chopin that he had heard through the windows, resurrected in him thoughts of his father many years ago. The deep longing for his home rose like barbed wire as he played back the past. Crying and inconsolable the little boy had been confused as to why he had to leave without his family. Why couldn't they take him on the train journey? But that was so long ago and he had made his life in England, never to see them again as Germany followed its traumatic course.

No children of his own and no family left, to whom could he entrust his precious violin? He chose someone who was amazing, knew its true worth and would cherish it. He could feel the passion that this child had for making music. Sarah was staggered that anyone could be so generous. The violin was obviously valuable, she knew enough from Alex's tuition to recognise its visual quality. Its maple back gleamed, banded by lighter sycamore wood. The spruce front led to a burnished maple and ebony fingerboard. Rosewood pegs and perfectly formed scrolls on the neck completed the exquisite effect. It was a violin of some substance and quality, enhanced by a bow of ebony and horsehair.

Sarah worried over the free acquisition, fully appreciating that, though Alex would approve of the violin, he might balk at the method of gaining it. Melanie was already using a full size model, cheaply purchased to help her to continue playing but it was nothing like this one. How could she refuse his unselfish offer when it so clearly meant a lot to him? The deal was done, Melanie would have it and in return Sarah insisted that he should give it to her personally and hear her first attempts to play it. The man could have no idea of the transformation in Melanie that this instrument precipitated. Her small glowing face in raptures at its beauty, held it lovingly as she listened to the tone. She hugged him and stayed in his arms for what seemed like eternity, man, child and violin.

The bond between the two musicians was to last, as Papa Levi became part of the family, a surrogate grandfather. It didn't matter that Alex disapproved Melanie had so few people that she trusted or relaxed with, that Sarah knew the relationship was right for everyone. The breakthrough in Melanie's confidence and trust was such a relief to Sarah. Everyday life eased and the hiccoughs and problems grew further apart. She accepted that Melanie was never going to be totally relaxed in large groups or share humour and fun alongside her friends. She was unable to make eye contact with them, often had one sided conversations and focussed on what she was interested in, unaware that they were mentally elsewhere. Her friends accommodated her quirks and tried not to gossip about how dumb she was in some instances, but so clever at the same time. Alex's arrangement of music tuition for Melanie was stalling, she was growing bored and frustrated at these sessions. The limitations and constraints of this teacher were becoming obvious to

Sarah. She looked around and discussed alternatives with Papa Levi. It had to be someone proficient, but with enough understanding to nurture the idiosyncrasies of Melanie.

It was Papa Levi who solved the problem and found the perfect match between student and teacher. The gossip machine of his local bowls group had whispered about a strange young man buying a house near the park. It was hinted that he had been someone famous, but was now retired from his career. They laughed at this man's hermit-like way of living, reclusive and unwilling to talk or reveal his background. Levi had him pointed out to him as he wandered through the park where he often sat and chatted to his friends. The sycamore tree was a favourite place for Levi, the affinity for this wood due in no small part to his beloved violin. Melanie now drew out the nature of this wooden shape with her bow. He speculated on the number of violins that could be made from this tree, possibly thousands! However alive it gave pleasure to countless generations.

Levi next bumped into the man at close quarters on one Sabbath at the synagogue. He seemed to recognise the face from somewhere, but his mind would not spit out the context. Worrying and tussling to extricate where he had seen him, at last came to fruition. His face was on the cover of the CD he played occasionally, a much younger, fresher version, but definitely the same. Daniel Cohen, tipped to be an outstanding soloist, this first CD was to be his only one. He had dropped from sight to the public.

Levi's personality wouldn't leave the matter to rest there. Probing into the hidden past of this young man was no easy task. He seemed to have dropped out of the music scene with surprising speed. Days of persistent investigation at last resulted in success. Daniel had suffered a mental breakdown. This had halted his appearances and successfully engineered his disappearance from the prying eyes of the public. He simply evaporated from the scrutiny or sympathy of those around him, only his family had been allowed to help. Further visits to the synagogue produced a nod or smile to be exchanged between the two men. A casual conversation between associates gave them the formal introduction Levi was waiting for. Several further awkward conversations finally led to a convivial atmosphere between them. Levi finally plucked up his courage, unable to contain himself any longer.

"I really admire your musicianship Daniel, I have your CD at home," he ventured.

Slowly, Daniel raised his eyes and a hint of a smile warmed his frozen face.

"Thanks, but I don't play anymore," his words hung in the air between them.

Using his considerable social skills Levi pursued the topic. The hesitant, awkward moment passed as common ground was found between them. The appreciation and love for music swept them along as they talked about mutually respected composers. The loose friendship developed into a trusted companionship of two musicians enjoying time together. Two people dear to him had so much in common, Levi knew he must bring them together. He didn't know how or when, but he was sure that fate was intervening through him. He began discussing his instrument with Daniel and how much he missed it. Daniel, intrigued that Levi had parted with it at all, listened to the story of the little girl with curiosity. He didn't doubt his friend's sincerity and that his generosity had spilt over for the child, but did she deserve it? Expensive violins were usually bought if you could raise the cash. More importantly, the general rule was that the privilege of owning such an instrument went hand in hand with expertise and an invitation to play it. Sometimes great violins were leased to potential maestros for only their musical lifetimes. Levi attempted to explain that this girl was exceptional, but the doubt written on his friend's face still hung there.

"Look, why don't you meet me at the park near you? I'll bring my violin and the girl. You won't think me quite so mad!"

Daniel was dubious, but he liked the old man and didn't want to seem churlish. He could spare him half an hour, after all he had grown to enjoy the old man's company. Talking about his first love, music, had reminded him of what he was missing. It had been out of his hands to stop playing but he was scared to start again! He didn't ever want to feel so bad again. The blackness and hopelessness had swamped him all those years ago. All the training and practising through the years hadn't protected him from the stress of performing. Graduating from the Royal School of Music, his talent had catapulted him into a solo career. He worked and worked to be worthy of the opportunities that sprang up. The isolation and focus needed exacerbated his feelings of failing. Musical pieces began to obsess him, driving him onwards, never giving him rest. Paganini's Spanish dances repeated in his head until exhaustion finally gave him a brief rest. Fame and the constant need to keep proving himself, to blank out the eyes of those waiting to see him fail, pushed him on relentlessly. He was gifted, but was rarely sure that he was good enough. Emotional lows began to increase and away from his family and home ties his mind faltered, blanking out the pain and he collapsed. Short on sleep and physically weak from infrequent meals, Daniel succumbed to the meltdown of body, mind and spirit. He was so thankful to his parents who had plucked him out of view as his nervous breakdown became known. They had comforted and screened him from prying eyes as he signed himself into a clinic.

The slow climb back to health was protracted and he avoided playing music, it was only in the last two years that he could listen without weeping. If he had turned his back on it, it wasn't consciously done, rather a conviction that his feelings were too raw to chance the melodies reaching his vulnerability. Levi's friendship had opened up a new chapter for Daniel, reintroducing him to favourite symphonies and concertos. He was far happier now and was adjusting to living alone again in his new home. Daniel noticed the trio waiting for him, long before they spied him striding towards them. If he was surprised at how young the small girl looked, he was immediately drawn towards the mother. Sarah must be older than himself, but she was trim and very attractive, even though tell-tale worry lines framed her eyes. Levi glossed over any formalities or awkwardness and encouraged the child to open up the violin case.

It was far more than Daniel expected, the violin was extremely handsome. He admired it and speculated at what might be the history behind it. He knew Levi had escaped to Britain from Germany at the start of the Second World War. The batch of youngsters aged between two and seventeen had arrived by train without parents or in most cases family. They had been fostered or assimilated into the Jewish community.

"What do you think Daniel, do you like the instrument?" Levi asked patiently, after a long wait for some reaction.

"It looks great, but you can never tell its worth until you hear the tone," he cautiously replied. Melanie couldn't bear the stranger's study of her precious violin, or his gentle fingering of the wood, a minute longer.

"It's beautiful, the most beautiful sound I've ever heard, just listen to it talk to you!"

She lifted it out carefully, placed it under her chin and began to play. Sarah, Levi and Daniel fell silent as the child stood under the branches of the tree, totally engrossed until she was finished. She didn't notice passers-by or dogs bouncing around the park, only the violin, the music and herself were of any consequence in that time or space. Daniel nodded to the other two, and casually asked,

"Why do you play the violin Melanie? I can see you love music but why this instrument?"

The precocity of Melanie was unnerving as her young face turned to Daniel to answer,

"I couldn't use any other, this is the one that fills me inside. I have to search for the notes and make them mine, so that it touches me here," she tapped her chest where her heart beat trembled at the audacity of explaining to this man.

Daniel didn't wonder any longer, about Levi's reasons for giving the violin to someone so young. Melanie's potential shone and had soared through the park for anyone to hear.

The three adults were to meet and discuss what to do for the best. Since Daniel had never formally taught music, he would need to establish a musical relationship with Melanie if he were to be of any use. Surprisingly, he found that he wanted to help. The child was different, fragile but strong; reluctant but willing; shy but precocious in her talent. The remit of teaching was open for pupil and teacher, Daniel followed the lead of Melanie where possible and augmented the holes in her learning as they cropped up. Gradually, as his confidence grew in this new sphere of music, he could see where to push Melanie's knowledge. She had accepted him reluctantly but, after watching and summing him up, as he demonstrated difficult pieces of music to her, she became enthralled. A perfect match had been accomplished. As the weeks grew into months, and the months into years, it seemed to Sarah and Levi that there were no problems they couldn't handle. Daniel insisted that Melanie's attempts at composing were formalised and transferred correctly in notation form and she revelled in seeing her patterns and ideas added to notebook after notebook. They played them together, altering and improving them without conflict, and with no hint of hard work for either of them.

Joining a youth orchestra was more difficult for Daniel to engineer. He felt strongly that Melanie would benefit from a fuller spectrum of musicians, although the social element might be a negative for her. He had voiced the idea several times but she evaded any reply. Sarah had unpacked the unwillingness of her daughter and her insecurities in large gatherings. After yet again a polite refusal from Melanie, Daniel summoned up all his tact to look at the idea in a new way.

"Melanie, perhaps you should think of an orchestra as members of a huge musical family. They complement and endorse each other. Violins are one part of the picture, they stand alone without the support of the whole family."

Melanie's reply flawed him for a second.

"I don't want to have a large family. I like being alone, it helps me find something special inside me."

"Well, consider this then," he countered. "I believe that each instrument is similar to parts of our body. The piano for instance, is the brain co-ordinating bass and treble, organising and unifying around other parts. The percussion are our pulses throbbing to different speeds and dynamics. Wind instruments, the lungs, steady and true, brass the...,"

"What about the strings then?" she eagerly interrupted, "what do they do?"

Daniel paused to look straight at Melanie.

"I think you already know. Strings find and make the notes to echo with your heart, they bring their sound to add to the soul of the music. How can a heart do this without the body to support it, to fatten the sound until it overflows everywhere?"

Melanie had no answer. It did make sense, her conviction was complete and final. The youth orchestra was to be a milestone in a more balanced life than her mother could have hoped for. Daniel's life also expanded and was more inclusive. He now tutored other young musicians and his reputation grew in the local community. The income from teaching supported and helped him fund other projects. He volunteered at the local school to promote more music so that all could participate. Sarah's interest in the clinic, using music as therapy intrigued him further. He couldn't reconcile his own illness and his extreme reaction to the very music he created. At these centres music was a resource against the exact weakness he suffered in his mind. His rejection had thrown out the healing properties because of self-imposed targets and ego-centric performances. It had taken far too long, he concluded, to reverse his flawed beliefs. Using the wisdom of hindsight, he needed to help the young people around him.

Meanwhile, Sarah was delighted that her course in music therapy had extended her skills and, though she found it difficult she persevered. Finding a post to use her new qualifications put the icing on the cake. She could work short hours around Melanie's school timetable and, as her daughter grew older, extend her time. Steve, her manager had helped by working the rotas in such a flexible way that at last it seemed the sun was shining upon her. She loved the work, revelling in any improvement that came with it for her patients. Steve was so willing to help, an unassuming facade hid a quiet, charming man. The antithesis of her husband, reliable, steady and most of all unaware of his abilities. The two had so much in common and their attraction flowered, under the watchful eyes of their colleagues.

On the few occasions Melanie had been in Steve's company, she relaxed in his casual style and contact was simple. There was no fear that her mum's time and obvious pleasure with him could attract attention away from herself. She could never conceive these thoughts or emotions. Mum was her bridge between the unfathomable or unknown, and where she flourished. The warmth and care Steve showed for Sarah began to thaw out the icy reserve she had built around herself. She had learnt not to expect help or love from Alex and so had showered all her love on Melanie with no time for self pity. Steve was careful not to intrude on the closeness of mother and daughter but filled in the blank spaces left by Melanie's detachment. Sarah's needs for reciprocal love couldn't be met in any tactile sense, but she knew that her daughter's disconnection was part of Asperger syndrome and not any indicator of lack of love. Eye contact and well chosen words, though given sparingly were pearls between them.

Steve slowly gained Sarah's trust and their mutual love grew until she couldn't remember a time when she didn't seek out his thoughts and ideas in her life. He had quietly grown to be her partner, loving and caring for her child, alongside awakening in her a love and a deep need for him. She had never felt love returned in equal measure without the demand for much more than was ever given back.

Both were free to marry, but there was one huge obstacle that needed to be overcome, Melanie's future. Steve had never married, due in no small part to being the sole carer for his disabled, autistic sister. After his parent's death he had automatically taken over the day to day logistics of her severe needs. The sparse free time he had between her schedule and his work gave no time for lasting friendships. That was all behind him now, for his sister had died. Sarah and he had met shortly after and he had felt no guilt in finding pleasure and happiness in her company.

"It's high time you enjoyed yourself mate," his friends would argue, "come and join us, we're going to Valentino's for a meal."

Steve would join them readily enough, but it would be some time as a couple before they could arrange anything spontaneously. Papa Levi had been invaluable as a frequent child-minder but they were careful not to misuse his good nature.

It was clear that Melanie would follow the music world when she left school. Her teachers were adamant that she could be equally successful in a career using maths.

Sarah and Steve had discussed the possibilities, but the real stumbling block didn't lie in what she studied, but rather how a stable home life could be achieved. Sarah worried about student life and how she would cope. Melanie's teenage years had been a series of peaks and troughs that were childish and nothing like her actual age. At the same time, her intelligence accelerated which placed her ready to study at university level at a very young age.

Daniel also was troubled that Melanie needed more than he could give her.

"She has such potential Sarah, I must keep her moving forwards. She'll get bored if I don't: I want her to study with the best!"

Together, they decided that she should try for a place in the Royal School of Music, knowing that the auditions would confirm or reject their own assessment. They would need to explain her position fully but they knew Melanie wouldn't be phased by the audition itself.

Daniel wrote to his old tutors and was pleasantly surprised at the warmth of their replies. Several of his contemporaries were now established staff members, and wanted to meet to catch up with his news. A few weeks later, his trip to London organised with appointments and meetings, had exceeded his wildest expectations. Not only was Melanie to be interviewed and auditioned but the strength of welcome from his former friends had amazed him. It showed how imperfect his reactions had been towards them during his breakdown. He went to his parents' home to show them his new found health and put their minds at rest. He mentioned Levi to them and they were eager to meet him, hoping to find common roots and background. Casual dinners and social times with his friends strengthened the tendrils of their common interests. In their company he realised what he had missed and his dry, cactus like existence was watered and nourished.

He revisited them as often as his teaching commitments would allow and Levi went with him on one occasion. Daniel persuaded his friend to meet up with his parents, as they were always asking after him. He was certain that if they didn't actually recognise each other, the association would benefit everyone. The stilted introductions were rapidly over and the three people explored their common backgrounds. It was clear that a deep sadness remained, as any child who had been plucked away from parents would retain. The natural alliance of fellow victims to survive soon propelled them into happier waters. Though they could only vaguely remember each other as children on that train station in London in 1938, they had a wealth of experiences to compare. All three had a joy of music running through their veins, as strong as lettering through a stick of rock. Levi had been lucky to be allowed to bring his father's violin, tucked under his arm for safety, knowing that the Germans would confiscate it if they thought it of any value. He knew it was the most precious gift his father could have given him. Learning to play it was a living tribute to a father he would never see again. A considerable time later, mouths dry from chattering and laughing, the three had put the world to rights again. Sarah, Melanie and of course Daniel were paramount in the conversations. Daniel's parents began to get an insight into how Melanie and Sarah had brought their son back into a more normal life. They felt a sense of gratitude and relief to both, but an enormous debt to Levi their new found friend.

Melanie held the printed letter tightly in her hand and read it for the hundredth time.

..."they were pleased to offer her a place to study the violin."...

The Royal School of Music wanted her to study with the maestros and professors! Her excitement had bubbled over when she showed Daniel the acceptance letter. He was delighted but she couldn't understand why he wasn't exploding like herself?

Wasn't she the one, Mum had explained, who needed to show when she was happy?

Well she was doing so now!

Why weren't the adults leaping around with the news?

They were glad, she could see that, but there was a wariness in their words. Sarah and Steve had smiled at her delight that morning when she opened the letter but, as normal, kept their responses cautious and metered.

Didn't they know she wanted this more than anything else in the world? Her Dad had told her that only the best would get a place. She knew she wasn't the best but they would see that it was her passion, surely?

Daniel had insisted on concentrating on the new piece she was learning before he would allow himself to scan the letter. They celebrated the triumph of the moment by playing an Irish jig and dancing round the room. Any caution or anxiety had been resolved for Daniel, he was convinced that the strategies hammered out by Sarah and himself should cover all eventualities.

"Come back tonight, Melanie, with your Mum, we've something to discuss with you together," he had finally thrown out as they packed their violins away.

"Get your Mum to phone me if she can't make it, but we do need to thrash out the details quickly." Melanie had never seen him so thrilled before, he was acting more like a boy than a tutor.

What Daniel didn't know was that her mum had already prepared her for the discussion ahead. Steve and she had broached with Melanie how she might go to London to study, and her future living arrangements. Papa Levi had even been involved as they sat around talking over the options of where Melanie would stay. She really didn't know what the fuss was about, it wasn't important, only what the course entailed mattered at all. She supposed Mum wanted to make it as easy as she could, so she would try and take part in the conversations.

Papa Levi had been the biggest surprise, he was selling up his lovely home to live in London again. It seemed his renewed friendship with fellow Jews, and particularly Daniel's parents, lured him back. The extra shock that Daniel and he were buying a house together puzzled her even more. How could he teach here as well as live in London? Mum explained that Daniel had been offered a teaching post at the Royal School of Music and that it was time he returned to where he had been happiest. The jigsaw pieces were starting to fit in a magical way. Melanie could live with Papa Levi and Daniel in term time, and Daniel's mother would help in running the household and keep an eye on Melanie's well-being. Daniel would continue to be her tutor, mentor and, most of all, her friend. Sarah carefully put the question to her,

"What do you think, Melanie, do you think you could be happy in their home?" Her daughter's features were inscrutable as usual and Steve wondered just how much she cared at leaving home. Her indifference would be tested when Sarah was no longer there as her backstop, smoothing the path ahead.

Steve had already reckoned on the impact upon Sarah and was working out a contingency plan that would keep them together as a couple, and permit their marriage to go ahead. The habits of fifteen years might drive Sarah to follow her daughter, especially since Daniel had offered her a room in his home. Steve suspected he was attracted to her but Sarah seemed oblivious and loyal to him. Still, he wasn't taking any chances, he had been making his own enquiries! There was a good job waiting for him in a fantastic clinic in London. His reputation had opened the chance for promotion and he was more than certain that Sarah could find a post there too.

Sarah had voiced that she wanted Melanie to try and settle on the course and in her new home without her. It was imperative that she had the space away from her mother's influence, but Steve wouldn't underestimate the massive vacuum for Sarah herself. He had to be there for her and perhaps wedding plans would be the ideal antidote. He would keep in hand the alternative he had found for Sarah and him to move to London. One step at a time, Melanie's transfer to London, their wedding and then what ever the future held for all three of them.

It was getting late, Melanie felt pangs of hunger, she needed to hurry as her mum would be getting dinner and she remembered Daniel wanted to see them tonight. Gathering her case tightly, she quickened her pace and left the park.

Notes of music were still to be heard in the early evening air as Melanie hummed her new music and left the bench. It was a familiar sound, contributing to the beauty around. The music blended with the renditions from the creatures who had practiced their early bird chorus in this same place. Sounds of insects and animals could be heard all day, if the human noises could be obliterated.

Melanie adored this place, to be quiet, to fuse the melody and harmonies of nature. It was a two way channel for, as she received its musical charms, she reciprocated and played it back. It entered her very core and replaced the failure to be average or normal.

The outside natural world was a bandage to the wounds that separated and excluded her from society. Music and creation made her whole.

Chapter 11

Dave

He had drifted off again when the jingle of keys nearby entered his unconscious state. The verger was locking up the church doors. It wouldn't be long before he padlocked the outer gates to prevent people like Dave sleeping there. The verger, a stout, older man was gentle in manner and speech when he approached Dave. It had been difficult and rather uncomfortable to refuse his offers of help. Dave knew he meant well but he had heard it all before. It was beyond him to explain it again to this stranger. What he needed couldn't be explained or excused. Right now he needed that golden warm liquid exploring his gut and restoring warmth to creaky limbs and throbbing forehead.

Limping along the pavement once more, he was relieved that his feet were now behaving themselves as circulation returned to his toes. Vaguely he considered his options. It was still too early to return to the park, he would easily be discovered by the park-keeper on his rounds in daylight. It needed to be twilight before he made his way there. Through the gloom surrounding his thoughts an idea surfaced- a small convenience store open for twenty four hours. Yes a few days ago, that was where he had found an unlikely source of free food. By accident he had passed that way around this time and noticed a youth filling up the bins. The overflow of packaging and products had been hastily pushed into the bin, probably against correct procedures. The youth, eager to finish his shift, wanted to get rid of these items speedily and without further trouble. Dave might find his supper there if he was quiet and unobtrusive. The air seemed thicker by the minute, surely there would be a storm soon.

He trundled along trying to keep his mind off the booze. It took him over so quickly. All his will had to be summoned. The fight weakened and exhausted him continually. Sometimes he couldn't think of anything else, the magnet drew him to tease and calculate how to get his next fix. This second voice in his head hissed and coaxed him, deceiving him, telling him, "just the one." Dave's small hoard of coins wouldn't buy him anything, he hadn't collected nearly enough. The hot drink that he could have bought wouldn't get rid of this overwhelming urge. Perhaps, he reasoned, food would fight the battle but if he spent it now what would he use for tomorrow lunchtime? Besides the small sum bought more at the Cornerhouse. He just had to make a little contribution, not pay for the whole price of the meal.

Dave noticed a bench in front of the shop next to a bus station. He was desperate to adjust his trainer, his toes cramped inside cried out for relief. The blood surged through, tingling and jarring as he wriggled his foot. Moments later, pulling on the trainer to his reluctant limb, Dave bent down to tie up the lace. A flutter of paper caught his eye, trapped near the leg of the bench. He retrieved it further to reveal a note, a ten pound note! Mesmerised for a second, it was some time since he had handled a note, he looked around. The area was quiet as people had already scurried home to prepare evening meals and go about their business. Even the shop itself seemed unusually devoid of customers. He clutched the note and turned it over. Yes, it seemed authentic, he thought for a moment it might have been some kid's Monopoly or play money.

It was his now. There was no obvious owner nearby even if he had wanted to return it. This was a lifeline thrown to him. There was no doubt what to use it for, the inner voice urged him on. Vodka was his solution to the demands of his body. Logically he would use it sparingly for medicinal purposes until he could see the doctor tomorrow. He convinced himself to go ahead.

Minutes later he left through the automatic doors of the shop, surreptitiously holding the bag. The half bottle would do the trick. He could hardly wait to feel the fiery liquid trickle down his throat. It would be better if he could find somewhere private to open it, somewhere he wouldn't draw attention to himself, it had proved a good practice in the past. Dave hurried now, with a spring in his step, to get to the derelict house he had passed earlier. Only a few minutes to hold on, round the corner and into the cul-de-sac.

The house stood further back than the others, a scorched relic from a former fire. No one seemed to be bothering with it, maybe waiting for an insurance claim. Walking through the small front garden, Dave hoped that the back would be private and unseen from adjoining neighbours. It was perfect, the garden banked by high fences and shrubbery couldn't be seen at ground level, though first floor windows might give a view. He found a suitable spot between an old shed and the rubbish bins. Slowly Dave unscrewed the top savouring the moment. His gut contracted again and his trembling hands fumbled. The craving for the taste was subordinate to the intensive yearning for relief in his stomach. He wished he could erase the disgust he felt for himself.

He swallowed, long and hard, at the bottle neck as a survivor in a desert might gulp his first taste of water.

Chapter 12

7.00 p.m.

Time was running out for Sophie in so many ways as she crossed the park to Granddad Keith's house. Her day at the hospital on the wards had been packed with problems and she was glad that she could leave it behind. She wondered if her hormones might be all over the place, but that didn't excuse her mistakes and shortcomings. Granddad was on her mind right now and his plans to chain himself to the sycamore tree the next day. She thought them stupid though well intentioned. He would land himself in a lot of trouble. If she could speak to him alone, she might be able to dissuade him from the whole idea. Especially if she suggested grandma Janet wouldn't like him putting himself at risk.

Sophie's bag was heavy with food for his meal that night. She thought that a meal might soothe and protect him from the unpalatable truths she would speak. The flash of inspiration had struck her on the bus journey home. She had jumped off at the next stop certain that the small supermarket would have what she needed. Keith loved lamb chops, it was his favourite meal. Unfortunately, her idea had turned out more expensive than it should have been! She was almost sure that was where she had lost her £10 note. Preoccupied with millions of thoughts, she must have been careless with her purse as she checked she had enough cash. There was no point in worrying about the loss, she was short of time and had more important things on her mind. Bob would be feeding the kids, she had left them a lasagne before leaving for work. He was really helpful at filling in when she was on late shifts, especially since Gran died.

Sophie hoped the meeting with the buyer had gone well, she knew how much it meant to him. Bob was growing more and more like his father these days, almost a workaholic. Where was her fun loving rebel of school days? She was pleased how consumed he had become by ambitions for his business. She knew how gratified his father must be that he had buckled down and was making a success of his work.

In contrast, Sophie was dismayed that time with the children was continually eroded. Peter was at an age where he wanted time with his dad. She was a poor substitute for football or sport though she was a willing supporter. Jane was easier to satisfy, glad to tag along beside her big brother. Sophie knew that she didn't give her enough attention and felt guilty about it. Was history repeating itself? She wanted to do better than her mother and give her time willingly, without reserve.

She couldn't help it, Peter's troubled face flew into her mind, recalling his latest words.

"Mum, why can't Dad take me after school tonight? Mr.Soames says he'll show a few of us how to race on the track at the Senior School."

"Maybe next time, Peter. Your Dad has got a very important time at work just now. It will get easier soon."

Her feeble excuses hung in the air. She could see his disappointment and resolved to turn down late shifts in the future so that she could take him. It often struck her that Dave, the natural father, was emerging through her son. Teachers had pointed out his aptitude in athletics and sport. Neither she nor Bob wanted to suppress them, they just needed to find more time. Over the last weeks Sophie had begun to detect a coolness between Bob and his son. Certainly there was tension in the home that she had to own as mostly her fault. Their ten year old marriage had survived despite the problems but recently Sophie had felt restless. Gran's death had uprooted her but the issue was more than that, she felt unappreciated, invisible, almost cellophane.

So many roles to play, could she have been an actress? What was she to Bob, wife, mother, secretary, accountant or general dogsbody? Where did friend or lover fit into day to day living? The fiery, consuming love of their teenage years had been quenched by practicalities. They were 'in love' but were they lovers anymore? She thought back to their school days, remembering an image of the three of them, Dave, Bob and herself. The love triangle that had caused their group of friends to take sides, to chose and pass judgement on her betrayal. Sophie remembered vaguely another picture of a much younger girl devotedly stalking Dave, her idol. What was her name? Emma? Something like that, she couldn't remember. If only Dave had turned to her when he was left alone. Perhaps things might have calmed down and prevented the uproar caused by herself and Bob. Sophie vividly remembered the pleasure she had felt when Bob had chosen her over all his admirers. Sophie realised what a contradiction it would have sounded if she had voiced her current resentment towards Bob. The one person she could have unloaded herself to wasn't around anymore. Gran's sensible ideas and pertinent comments were now only inside her own store of memories. Gran would have put things into perspective, she had done so all of Sophie's life. How she missed her!

She was comforted that the last, serious advice from Gran had confirmed her own views. Bob and she had always thought that it was right, at some time, to tell Peter that Dave was his natural father. At what point in his life, they hoped would be self-evident. Gran had counselled them that they shouldn't leave it much longer. It would be an enormous shock for his teenage years to digest. Together they had decided that the finish of the Junior School period would be the ideal time. Carefully selecting a weekend, they had sat down with Peter one evening after Jane was safely asleep. Bob had taken the initiative and tentatively explained how they had met as teenagers. Patiently he drew a picture of their circle of friends and Dave's part in the group.

It was easy to talk about love and friendship with Peter, as biology lessons had covered sex and conception at school in an objective setting. The reception to this personal revelation wasn't clouded by raging hormonal development or demands of his young body.

Peter's immature mind tussled with the whole idea of another man as part of his life. A stranger who was part of him and gave him genes and life? Yet he hadn't bothered to stay around and get to know him. He turned from Sophie to Bob, confusion rife on his face and body. Where was this man now? Did his real father know about him? Sophie's fumbled explanations were harder than she had anticipated. The evasions and lies behind the truth over the years had multiplied the difficulties. Anxious to protect the boy, they had omitted certain facts and avoided specific questions. Bob was his real father, in every sense but blood, and their only motives had been to keep Peter from harm. Wave after wave of questions on grandparents, aunts, uncles and cousins washed over them. Everyone became thrown into the melting pot of Peter's life. Which part of the family was secure for him? Half of the people he had grown up with were no part of his blood relations. His family had been sliced in two. Most of all, how did Jane fit into this reconstruction? Was she still his sister? No, she was better than that, she had both a mum and a dad! Sophie would never forget the hardest question of all.

"If you say you loved my real dad, then how can you have loved him?" He turned to Bob, "how can she have loved two people at the same time?"

Silence swirled around them, the familiar setting did nothing to mask the awkwardness. Sophie wrestled with the answer. All of Sophie's experience couldn't provide a resolution that would be good enough for that question. How could she clarify the circumstances, to explain her youth and naivety? She had always felt the blame and now was confronted by her son. She faced it accepting that he would judge her choices.

She asked herself, did she really choose either of them? Wasn't it more a case of reacting to others, following her personality, rather than choosing? Dave's quiet aura had shone through in the group with which she associated. It would have been unusual for him to push himself forward, he was just glad to be included. Quietly, he could always eclipsed others in sport but she liked him more for his lack of conceit. Sophie couldn't imagine what it must be like without parents, she wanted to look after him, rescue him from wasting his future prospects. The love she felt for him was warm, soft and comfortable. Bob invaded that fuzzy, easy companionship with vibrant, witty dialogue. He dominated the group and caught her attention and she came alive in the fun that surrounded him. His confidence and sunny nature captivated her and won her heart. Sophie made no attempt to unpack her feelings of empathy for Dave to Peter, or explain Dave's loneliness without parents. She made no excuses and had never admitted to herself even, the differences between the two men or her role in the mess they had created. Like a spider she had spun a web of selfless love for Dave that climaxed into one passionate evening.

"Where is my real dad now? I want to meet him," Peter demanded.

Glancing at Bob's withdrawn expression, Sophie swallowed hard. At that moment she felt she was losing both of the men who mattered most to her.

"Peter, we'll try and find your dad. We've tried before, but now you can help us." Sophie's answer would satisfy him for now, but she knew there was plenty to explain about their previous efforts to track him down.

Dave had understandably cut off all contact with Bob and Sophie after their relationship had been uncovered. It was only a matter of weeks before he had left school, signed up in the army and was sent away on basic training. In that short time he refused to talk or listen to any of his friends, turning away help or friendship. He vanished from the neighbourhood as neatly as the sea sucks in the seaweed.

Sophie waited until school was well over and, as her pregnancy became more visible she turned to her Gran. Her mum, Helen, had prised out of her daughter the truth of the impending birth, oblivious to all the facts. She had disguised the disappointment of her dreams for her daughter to her husband Barry, who always camouflaged his true feelings. They had met Bob and could see how much in love the pair were, they needed to give their support, no matter what lay ahead.

"What would Mum say, Gran, if I told her Bob isn't the father?" Sophie had blurted out round the table at her grandparents' home.

"I can't bear to see the look on Dad or Mum's face! They've just got to know Bob, how can I tell them what I've done?"

Gran and she worried over the problem until Sophie convinced her that the first priority was to find and speak to Dave. Dave's home at his Nan's seemed unwelcoming as she trembled on the doorstep. The hostile stare from the older, grey haired woman further reduced her courage, as she lowered her eyes to Sophie's belly. Nan refused to give out any information on Dave's whereabouts or even assure Sophie that she would let Dave know that Sophie wanted to contact him.

"What good would speaking to my grandson do? Haven't you messed him up enough?"

It seemed to Sophie they were both avoiding the obvious question or did Nan refuse to consider that the baby might be Dave's child? She had retreated without further words, absolutely sure it wasn't fair to stress or upset her further. Nan had no one to calm her fears, it was a secret that Sophie must hide for now. Tearfully, Sophie returned to her Gran's realising the bleakness of the mess. There was no clear solution after hours of talking with Bob and discussing the options. They added up the dates and came to a firm conclusion that it was Dave's baby. Sophie had no doubts, they had blossomed from virgins together to the adult world on that fateful date. Bob saw no obstacle, he loved Sophie and he would love her child as his own. They would get married and he would be a father.

Gran as usual, provided a solution for Sophie and the unsolved problem of Dave. Janet had met Nan, and knew her slightly from the local W.V.S. It might be possible to strengthen the link, time might heal and make her receptive to Sophie. As events turned out the idea couldn't be explored further, for Nan's death had put an end to this forlorn hope. Sophie remonstrated with herself that she ought to have found a way to reach Dave before Nan's death. It should have been a priority. There were no excuses, but many plausible reasons why it didn't happen. Day to day routines of a new baby, marriage and setting up a home and business had exhausted the young couple.

The months and years flew by until once again she was in hospital for the birth of their second child, Jane. Complications of high blood pressure had necessitated a lengthy period in hospital. Gran had brought the news, after the birth, that Dave had returned for the burial of his grandmother and disappeared again. Bob and Sophie's disbelief and clear disappointment at missing this opportunity caused eyebrows to be raised within the family, especially between Helen and Barry.

The truth was well overdue, Sophie needed her parents' acceptance of this secret. Their little family was secure and should be happy without hidden issues.

It was no surprise that Helen was upset, the secret tryst between her daughter and mother bowled her over. How had she been so far removed from the full extent of Sophie's dilemma? It wasn't comfortable for Sophie to describe, even now. Sophie had clearly felt so ashamed and thought she had let her mum down, desperately wanting to please and make her mum proud. Her father, Barry, and Helen had listened to Sophie as a child and her dreams for a medical career, a university degree, perhaps a place to study as a doctor. Her parents' partnership was a constant in her life, Helen with drive and purpose in tandem with the loyal support of Barry. Her father wouldn't have blamed her if she had chosen a different path to a career but she was scared to show him her foolishness. Helen and Barry consoled themselves with the thought that they had helped and accepted Bob without reserve. The early years of their daughter's marriage had been hard for everyone. Helen hoped that Sophie knew they were not sitting in judgement.

The relief that the whole family could now know the truth of the parentage of Peter wasn't as liberating to Sophie as she had anticipated. There was still the question of how to find Dave. The Army were experienced at deflecting details. When Sophie tried to find out about his enlistment it seemed that, outside of blood ties, she had few rights or avenues to explore. They had given her phone numbers which referred her to various other links. Most of the calls were passed onto others, or worse still, they offered to call back. She wondered where her letter to Dave was now. Filed away in some cabinet, disposed of in a bin, perhaps worse still, read and dismissed by Dave himself. Her futile early attempts discouraged her and it was easy to give up and wait for a better time, persuading herself that something would crop up. Now these recent demands of Peter to meet his dad, hung over Sophie further. To make matters worse, Bob didn't want to talk about it. She guessed he was hurt that Peter was asking to meet Dave so urgently. Rationally, Bob should have seen that nothing had changed Peter was still as loving and challenging as sons can be. He had adjusted to this rearrangement of his family surprisingly well. Bob was the only father he had ever known, the bond was strong but now complicated.

Once again Sophie asked herself, how can you miss the man you married when you're living with him? Where had he moved to? Or was she the one that had moved away? Her thoughts kept resurfacing and pounding away inside her head as she pummelled them down. She wondered if they were painted on her face, revealed in her eyes. Bob, obviously hadn't noticed much difference in her or was he ignoring the change? Perhaps he couldn't handle yet another problem in his family. Sophie couldn't gauge her success rate in hiding this new secret. She had hidden the signs from herself until compelled to face the truth of the pregnancy test. It had read positive.

This new life that was confirmed and real was absorbing and melding into her being. Hormones were rebalancing and adjusting to nurture its welfare outside of her control. Sophie took stock of her body reacting to stabilise this child, mothering was not new to her or unexpected. However the battle within her heart and mind was inexplicable. When she had looked at the colour change in the window of the cylinder she had been appalled at the mixture of emotions raging inside her. How could she not want this child?

"Sophie the carer, the nurturer, the epitome of Mother Earth overwhelmed with conflicting sentiments!" a sneering voice echoed inside her. She had hidden the evidence well away in the dustbin until she felt able to think further and give herself time. Sophie had experienced the dilemma of a crossroad once before and here she was again. At sixteen she had felt unequipped to make decisions that would lead her down the paths she must follow. Now she was in the same place, choices that would alter her life and those around her and she felt she wasn't ready or able!

Prior to these last few weeks, Sophie had been thinking of enrolling on a course to become a counsellor. The restless moods at work had made her realise she needed something more. People had told her she was a good listener and non-judgemental. This course intrigued her, it might be the perfect niche. Until now she had organised her work life around the priorities of home life. What she needed had always been subservient to the needs of others. Any career had been limited. Sophie had planned on leaving her job. After all, Bob was earning more these days, she didn't need to contribute. She could enrol on the course and still maintain home life for the family. So far she hadn't mentioned it to anyone. It was still in the embryonic state she mused, alongside the real one.

She must rethink now, she really could do with talking it over with someone urgently. Helen's face popped into her mind. The death of Janet had fused the two of them together in mutual grief. Even more than that, it released the mother and child roles between them so that they interchanged frequently. Swapping roles of comforter and comforted strengthened their bonds, Sophie wanted to speak to her mother as soon as possible. Helen was clever at thinking around a situation, she might be able to suggest how to pursue finding Dave. Sophie was tired of the closed doors and hurdles put before her. She had been at the mercy of circular phone calls on official sites. Helen might know how to access records that she hadn't thought about, she reflected that her mum was very resourceful.

It was wonderful how much happier Sophie felt now that she had made a plan. She hated feeling out of control, her gloomy moods weren't fair on the family. She touched her stomach and felt cosy and at peace. Helen's words from long ago, reminded her of how content she was when she first held Peter and then Jane in her arms.

"There's nothing that can compare to the completeness of having a child."

The wisdom of her mother hadn't gone unnoticed by Sophie when she considered Helen's career. She had, as an immature teenager, believed her mother had rated personal fulfilment over everything. Now she accepted that her mum, like herself, could handle several roles, their diversity gave freedom. The only chains around her were ones of love.

Keith sat in his favourite chair, fully satisfied by the meal Sophie had cooked. The lamb chops had been delicious, Sophie was an excellent cook and he had enjoyed her company. Eating alone wasn't fun and the gap left by Janet at the table, forced his loss to be accepted. He looked across at Sophie and recognised the familiar glint in her eyes. Just like Janet's expression, he could guess what was coming. Janet's common sense and practical nature had caused many debates and arguments over their years. He knew he was impetuous, that she had helped to curb his actions which caused trouble. Sophie had stayed for a last cup of tea and Keith waited to hear what was the real reason for her visit, as they sat down together.

Outside, noises from the park floated through the open window, the stormy atmosphere was coming to a peak. Thunderstorms had been forecast for that day, it wouldn't be long now, Keith concluded. However, the evening country calls and sounds were drowned out by angry human voices in the twilight. The park was coming alive, sounding more like a battlefield than the haven of peace Keith loved.

Huge, black mushroom clouds burdened the sky above the tree and bench, ignored by Sophie as she had turned into granddad Keith's home. Sophie's love of this park and tree could be traced back to all of her life.

It was part of her childhood and security, as much as her parents and grandparents. The roots of her family were as inseparable as the roots of this tree. Picnics, parties, holiday time from school, the tree had been an integral part.

If the tree was to be cut down, how would it effect her security? Can you miss a hole in the panorama? Weren't these the binding roots or permanency of the status quo, exactly what Sophie had been struggling against?

Her recent escalation of emotions left her undecided on the tree's future. She was glad she didn't have to make the decision.

Chapter 13

A slimy, wet and warm surface worked its way over his mouth, nose and eyes. Long, silky, savouring strokes allowed the dog's saliva to soak up the strange taste of the sugary alcohol, mixed with sweat on Dave's face. Contact moved to his hands and fingers, cleaning up any remnants of anything edible for the retriever. This unexpected source of free food rewarded the dog's persistent obsession and driving force. Through bleary heavy eye lids, Dave could make out a hairy face and wet nose that blew steam onto him. Realisation was slow, he couldn't place those liquid brown eyes into his dream. The vodka bottle was wedged under his hips, the last dregs soaked into the earth beneath him. His mouth stank from the coated veneer of spirit and remnants of his lunch. He remembered he'd finished all the vodka and was exasperated at his weak will. A long gulp of water was what he longed for now, clean, fresh and cold.

Sensation now was returning to his lower legs and feet from the awkward position of his sleep. His stomach had stopped cramping but the pounding in his head obscured any minor aches and pains, obliterating everything but this drum in his head. Dave realised that he'd forgotten what it felt like to have a comfortable body. He was forced to give attention to the increasing pain that controlled his entire days. His father's words surfaced again,

"Your body is the vehicle for your future."

He could picture him now, muscular and toned, thriving and energetic, ready to face whatever was thrown at him. How ironic that he was dead, fatal events taking precedence over any fitness regime, disproving theories of a long life. Dave contrasted himself against his dad. He was the living proof that abuse to yourself doesn't always shorten a life span. There were many times he'd wished it did! True, he'd alternated between prolonging his life and giving up, but the fact was clear, his body was in a mess and yet he still survived.

He pulled himself up into a sitting position and stretched his arms and stiff shoulders. The dog had moved onto rummaging in the dustbins without success. They were filled with wood and debris from the house. A distant voice rang in the air calling a name. The dog looked up and carried on, intent on filling the void inside. Dave struggled to his feet, patting the animal as it sniffed around his feet and bag. It was friendly enough and he enjoyed the warmth and silent affection it gave him.

"Stay boy, heel," an authoritative voice interrupted the silence, "what do you think you're doing, mate?" the man turned to Dave as he grasped the dog's collar. They eyed each other suspiciously. Dave held eye contact for a split second before dropping his stare and shuffling away. He hadn't meant any harm, he was just patting the animal. Did the man think he was going to hurt or take him away? A surge of anger and heat fuelled his body, the stickiness of the air added to the intensity around him. He made no answer, he'd found it easier to back down in similar situations. His befuddled state from the short nap didn't help, he wanted to avoid trouble.

"This is private property, I don't think you should be here," the man continued, "they're starting work soon, so you can't stay."

By this time the dog was pulling hard on the lead, anxious to be off to explore new places. Together they turned away with a last word from the man,

"Make sure you're gone before I get back, or I'll have to notify the police that you're trespassing."

Dave sighed, his last breath emptying the deflated balloon sensation deep within himself. His clothes stuck to his skin. The result of fear perhaps, or a reaction to the alcohol? He couldn't guess which. Certainly, the humidity had grown as the impending storm was now threatening the slate grey sky. The sun hidden by cauliflower clouds struggled to assert itself.

Maybe he would be in luck, evening twilight would be early. The park would empty if this storm materialised and he could settle down unobserved. He knew how to combat the elements, his plastic sheet would work to solve getting drenched, particularly if he could use the natural protection of the tree's branches. He would get out of this garden quickly before the man and his dog returned. His tongue was parched, urging him to find water, the dehydration effects were worsening. He knew where to find it, the park could satisfy his twin needs of water and shelter. The drinking fountain placed near the small remaining formal gardens was a remnant of former times in the park. He must hurry, his thirst edged him on. Convinced he would return to the park, where he would spend the long night ahead, Dave gathered his few possessions and made his way out of the garden and street to return to the starting point of his day.

Chapter 14

8.00 p.m.

Harry dragged his heels, reluctant to go any further into the park grounds. He didn't want to be there or do what he'd set up that day. He would put an end to the knot in his stomach and the heaviness that descended on him on waking this morning. The dread of this meeting with Mick had haunted him all day but he had no choice to accept it and go ahead.

The sky, now an inky grey, was a contradiction to the rising temperature as each second heralded the storm about to break. A few heavy drops of rain plopped on his shoulders and then evaporated as quickly, waiting for fellow companions to join in the torrent that was threatening. Harry's tee shirt clung to him, large patches of sweat growing under his armpits as the adrenalin pumped in his blood stream. Mick would be waiting for him, probably with his cohorts to witness his humiliation. Harry couldn't rationalise that any weakness of his was only an imperfect reflection or mirror image of the utter shame that his sister felt. Harry considered the huge impact on Becky his sister since they had moved here six months ago.

Elenor, his mum, had found their new home well away from the hurt and pain of their old address. Since his dad had died of cancer she had fought to make a new start for the four of them. The struggle of the long illness and necessary nursing had reduced all the childrens' resilience but especially her own. After the first three months following his death, his mum had, step by step, hauled the family into looking ahead.

A new start where they could afford the rent and good schools nearby should herald a future to anticipate. Harry, Becky and Ruth held a family conference with mum and agreed the decision was practical and should have many advantages.

Ruth had settled into Junior School without effort or hindrance. Six years younger than Harry, she made friends easily and had joined school clubs becoming almost part of the fixtures. Her mother had been grateful that the transfer had been easy for her youngest child. Losing a father when so young caused her to worry about the impact on Ruth more than her elder two children. She was lucky herself, finding work in a local supermarket where she could juggle the shift times around. Elenor was confident that the move to this new place was proving a success. She had no idea what her eldest son and daughter were going through and hiding from her.

Harry, a lanky, spotty youth of fifteen had kept to himself in the first days of starting the new school. He watched and carefully took stock of the different groups within his year and class. He didn't belong to the sporty crowd and although fairly brainy, didn't want to be included with the nerds. Other disparate gaggles of teenagers herded together following one interest or another. He wasn't interested in girls, two sisters were quite enough for him at this stage, but he could just about tolerate them in a mixture of friends. Slowly he was assimilated into a bunch of obsessive music buffs, who hung out together ear plugs blaring out as they followed the latest hits. Harry began to relax and enjoy the time they spent together particularly when the eldest and tallest, Phil, took him under his wing. He was now part of a group, happy in their company and so grateful to Phil that he had been included. Harry admired everything about him. He was more than a friend, someone who had become almost a hero, maybe a soul mate.

The turmoil of his attraction towards another boy couldn't be understood or dismissed. He pushed it out of his mind, it was unthinkable. More worrying than his hidden thoughts, he wondered if he was showing his feelings. The changes of puberty were accelerating and with it the numerous dilemmas, questions and problems that he had no one to share with or discuss. He would have given anything to chat with his dad just one more time. His father might not have had the answers but he knew he would have listened and they would have laughed at the absurdity of his curiosity. Now he had to assume the role of the alpha male for the sake of his mother and sisters. They needed him to grow up and fill the vacuum left by his father. It didn't matter that Becky was older, for the first time he felt the weight of his own expectations, to look out for the family.

So far, no one in his year group had noticed anything peculiar about him. Harry had guessed that it wouldn't be disregarded, the Twitter brigade would have exposed him without hesitation. He pored over various Facebook pages frequently, to make certain he wasn't the subject for speculation or innuendo. It was important that he spoke to no one until he could sort himself out and come to a certainty on his sexuality. Scrolling through the Facebook site two months ago he found himself onto a page belonging to Sally, a girl in his year group. It was full of the usual girlish chatter but a name jumped out of the screen, Becky Selland.

What was she doing talking about his sister? He didn't think that they knew each other, Becky was a good two years above him or his class mates. Of course, Sally's sister was in the same year as Becky, maybe that was the connection. Harry paused, staring again at the text,

'She's weird, my sister says at her last school everyone knew she was a slag!'

He closed down the computer, his mind tossing around. What to do next? Becky was in her room doing her homework, as usual. She spirited herself away after dinner, studying for the summer exams, rarely spending time with anyone since they had moved here. In fact, now he thought about it, she had altered these last months.

Becky had always been fun, laughing and giggling with her younger brother and sister. She was the one who would play pranks and make games of the most boring chores. A ray of sunshine that had melted the misery of the protracted illness which shrouded the family. After their dad's death, her support and practical solutions raised even mum's spirits in the first difficult days. Reluctantly, he admitted to himself that she was quieter, loath to go out and ready to excuse herself from family plans.

Homework and the impending exams were hard enough but she pointed out that extra private study was important if she was to fit into the new sixth form at such a late date. Elenor was afraid that their decision to move was rebounding in a disastrous manner on her daughter. It was too late now! Becky assured her it was getting easier, she just needed to focus on her work.

Harry's worries niggled away until he couldn't wait any longer. Finding a perfect opportunity when Mum and Ruth had gone out, he tapped on Becky's bedroom door.

"Go away, I'm busy. What do you want?"

He persisted knocking until she was forced to open it. Her face was tear stained and ashen but still angry with him for the interruption.

"I told you I'm busy, go away. I need to finish this," her eyes travelled to the untidy piles of books and blank computer screen. It was obvious that studying was the last thing on her mind, her bed warm and messy from where she had lain.

Harry had never credited himself on having any tact or sensitivity, but somehow he was in the right place with the exact words for Becky. Slowly and hesitantly the truth spilled out of those weeks after enrolling at the school. Harry and Becky were alike in many ways, avoiding the limelight until they were confident in their new surroundings. Becky had always been popular with her age group, slim and an emerging beauty, she was liked by the boys and copied by the girls

No one could have called her a follower of fashion, she thought of clothes and make-up with realism. Her image wasn't controlled by stars and celebrities. Assured in her own skin, she might have generated envy with others and sometimes did. Usually the jealousies were minor and with her natural sunny nature she managed to solve the problems. At the new school it was harder, the ethos in the sixth form wasn't inclusive to latecomers. Girls eyed her suspiciously and held back from encouraging her into any group. One or two boys viewed her optimistically, but were deterred by her apparent aloofness. Her confidence ebbed away further and she drew back content to wait.

Texting flew between the young people, speculating and hinting at her background. They scrutinised her dress style, hair and mannerisms until they could find a tag to name her. Nerd, Chav, Emo they couldn't put her in any pigeon hole, she was just WIERD. Ideas began to fester and take root. Rumours flourished where knowledge was scarce and became facts in their own right.

Becky's Facebook page grew and friends multiplied in an attempt to discover anything. She was part of the texts, tweets and inboxes flying between them. At first they helped her feel she was being accepted, she happily shared her photos and memories of the past. She willingly gave out details, innocently believing they were interested, until gradually, the innocuous ramblings turned into slanging matches. Gossip and innuendos were replaced by a web of lies. It was unbelievable how simple facts could be skewed and turned into an unrecognisable past event. She dreaded logging on each day, but daren't leave it idle!

The computer, the source of the hurt and pain, multiplied the damage a hundredfold. She didn't want to know the false comments and fabrications made up by the bullies, but was compelled to find out the worst. Sometimes she knew the person causing the trouble but often the anonymity of remarks hurt her more.

Becky distrusted her whole world and was always reading the faces around her and looking for deceit. The bullying took over her life, gobbling her every minute. She searched for answers. How had they got hold of those old innocent photos taken at the last school? Which so called pal had passed them on? She hardly recognised the carefree, laughing girl, arm in arm with boys and girls from her old class. How did this make her 'a tart', a girl who would 'put out for anyone?' Dare she wear that new skirt, did it make her look like that? Becky now so insecure, doubted everything she did and took sanctuary within herself. She cried herself to sleep, longing for her father's arms around her and the hugs he would have given so freely. Urged on by the girls, the boys singled her out for suggestive invitations to dates or parties. She refused immediately and shied away from contact. Her isolation prevented any normal chatter, or hands of friendship between others, to be seen as such.

Harry had listened, alarmed but mesmerised by these tales, it hadn't occurred to him that his sister was in such trouble. Becky had been so careful to disguise her embarrassment, so clever to hide the truth. He was sure his mum wasn't aware of any of the problem and she was adamant that it remained hidden. It was the latest development of Becky's misery that bothered him most, the addition of Mick onto the scene.

The gang around Mick were well known to Harry though they were slightly older than him. They were well known to everyone as tough and troublesome if you got on the wrong side of them. Mick, their leader, had a bad reputation with staff and pupils alike. They feared his temper, fists and power. He had started appearing at odd times and places where Becky had to pass. Silently watching her, leering and smiling to himself. Sometimes his mates gathered nearby, muttering and sniggering at jokes, probably at Becky's expense. She only knew that wherever she went she was followed from room to room, building to building. There seemed to be an endless stream of stalkers but most of all Mick was noticeably visible. A spooked Becky couldn't think clearly, only wonder where he would turn up next. She changed her routes, times and habits but it didn't make much difference. He followed her home whichever route she chose, she sensed him near, watched for him. The word was out, it sped electronically that Mick had singled Becky out. Speculation mounted. What could you expect? Everyone knew what she was, just right for Mick.

Harry tried to diffuse the effect that Mick had on Becky as soon as he knew everything. He met her as often as possible and walked her to school in the morning. It caused curiosity in his own circle of friends but he took the blame readily enough, anything to divert attention away from Becky. What did it matter if they sniggered at his close attachment to his sister? He countered the sneers and chants from Mick's groupies by turning up the volume of music on his headset. Sometimes he was amazed at himself, he didn't rate himself highly on the courage scale but the need to take over his father's role spurred him on. Days passed and whatever tactic he used to mitigate the bullying, didn't seem to work. It was slightly better now for Becky that the two of them were involved in the situation, the trouble was shared. Harry sensed that, while she appreciated his futile efforts, she had to concentrate on the final exams, they were her ticket to escape.

As a last resort Harry came up with a plan that he would keep secret from Becky until he'd succeeded. He set about arranging a date between Becky and Mick using her Facebook page. He knew her password, he would email Mick so that only he could see, lest the message be relayed to Becky. Harry intercepted the reply and fixed the time and place, it needed to be soon as he would have to find a way to put his sister's computer out of action. He couldn't risk her finding out, she would have stopped the whole scheme. He gambled on no one contacting her. It was such good luck that Mum had arranged a late night shopping spree with his two sisters. Everything was falling into place. Then, as a last security measure for his plan, Harry deleted the messages concerning the meeting.

Harry calculated that an appeal to Mick's greed might put a stop to the stalking. He would pay protection money to Mick to stamp out the bullying of Becky in the school. He hadn't given away his thoughts and Mick seemed eager to meet with Becky even assuring her he would get rid of his mates and be alone. Harry had to hope it would all work.

Chapter 15

9.00 p.m.

Mick tapped his toe, jiggling his leg on the bare earth repeatedly. He was tense, it was a habit that his friends had witnessed many times and joked about. Gang members sprawled around in small groups, desperately trying to keep cool in their army camouflage jackets. It was absurd in this heat to dress so heavily, but they must use their unofficial uniform. People recognised their authority and gave them a wide berth. They passed around beer and cider cans in an attempt to slake their thirst, to reduce the sweat in this clammy atmosphere. Mick ignored them, he'd just wrestled words with Tommo, sneering at his leader for hanging around this dump of a park. Mick recognised that Tommo was waiting for a chance to take over the gang at the first opportunity or sign of weakness. His best mate wouldn't hesitate to seize the moment. It didn't matter, he was anticipating the look on their faces when 'she' turned up! No one had dared to voice their opinions on his obsession with Becky. He knew they were laughing at his persistence with 'the tart' and her wierdo brother, surely there were other more amusing victims.

He couldn't speak of his true feelings. Becky had reached a part of him that he'd never imagined he possessed. She was frail and he felt tenderness towards her, he wanted to defend and protect her. She lacked confidence and he wanted to be her protagonist. Mick's understanding of these conflicting emotions was well outside his normal thoughts and experience. He liked the way she handled all they could throw at her, she had a presence that couldn't be penetrated. His admiration grew inch by inch and he wanted more. So she didn't come to any harm, Mick would watch out for her and get to know what she liked and where she went. He convinced himself completely that his actions were for her benefit, even when she so clearly hated his appearances. She seemed to look for him, perhaps that indicated she found him attractive. Secretly, he felt Becky viewed him as a thug, after all he'd spent his whole life building this tough image. Why would she be attracted to him? It was only girls who emulated the same coarseness that hung around the gang. Mick's stomach rumbled, he was hungry and there was no food at home, he'd filled the void with the only thing available, beer. On his return home he'd found his dad sprawled out in front of the TV snoring loudly, beer cans lying empty on the floor. No work to use up his time, his dad had resorted to filling up his days drinking at the pub. Released from prison he'd been a shell of the once strong and often violent man of his younger days. Widowed years ago with a parcel of four sons to look after, he'd wrestled at the mountain to climb, bringing up three small boys and Mick, a new baby. They needed a mother desperately but his pride shunned any offers of help.

Dad had done his best. Mick remembered the culinary attempts which occasionally appeared on the table. The overflowing dirty laundry and squabbles between his brothers as they fought to regain underwear or anything clean. There was no moderating influence to stop the fights and physical damage on each other. Survival of the fittest was the mantra of the brothers and, as the runt of the litter, Mick couldn't hope to compete.

His oldest brother, Doug, would occasionally defend Mick when he was small but pushed him to toughen up and stop whingeing. It was lucky that their dad's prison stint for grievous bodily harm didn't split up the family. They were now old enough for social services to allow them to stay as a unit. Mick had been relieved to live with his older brothers in the family home. Even though they ordered him around he wanted to be with them. Losing both a dad and a mum, Doug became a rock to him, his security. It was all the harder to bear when, at the first chance Doug emigrated. Mick didn't blame him, he could understand the reasons why, but it didn't soothe the hurt he felt at being abandoned. Perhaps Doug couldn't stand the troubles that rained down from his other brothers, Geoff and Kyle.

Geoff was violent to anyone and everyone around him. He had to keep proving to the world he was someone. The loss of a mother had coloured him and he desperately needed his dad to notice him and be proud. The step by step progress to a life of petty crime went unchecked until prison swallowed him up into the system. The disinterest of anyone to halt events forged a steely, hard young man that couldn't be reached.

Kyle and Mick, now left with an aging dad, managed as best they could. Kyle funded the household bills alongside his dad's meagre benefits. Mick had stopped worrying about money recently. He knew Kyle did occasional work but the details were sketchy and usually avoided in conversation. His dad wasn't concerned, so why should he be bothered? Several times he'd found Kyle slumped unconscious in his room and knew it wasn't alcohol induced. Kyle had laughingly shown his brother varying drugs and designer pills. Mick knew not to ask the source. It didn't take a genius to realise his brother was involved in the drug scene but he couldn't take the risk of being dragged into the mess. Mick was counting the days to leaving school desperate to find some legal way to make money. Work beckoned and he didn't care what kind, only to get enough to be independent. He hated feeling weak and reliant on others in the family. At school he learnt quickly to take power off weaker kids, growing in stature through force. It was so easy, they were feeble and controlling them was what he'd learnt so effectively through his home. He became the leader of a tough gang, naturally commanding and managing those around him. His bullying tactics multiplied as he applied his brother's techniques. Mick stamped out any rising hints of sensitivity when he saw the tears and pain in his victims. The weakest link in his family, he was ready and able to attack, to emerge as an impressive predator at school. He was so successful, an era of dominance hid the real Mick.

Through the mire of hate it was amazing that he had noticed Becky at all. He actually wanted to rescue her from the cycle of cyber-bullying, rumours and gossip. Childhood fantasies of being a knight rescuing his princess from a dragon were tossed out of his mind as stupid. Yet here he was, waiting for her, uncomfortable in the heat, hungry and drowning his nerves with beer. In his heart Mick knew he'd wait for her however long it took, she filled his thoughts in daytime and entered his dreams at night. It had been unbelievable that the meeting was arranged, he'd built the moment up time and time again. He couldn't believe his luck!

Tommo's peevish voice interrupted his fantasies,

"What are we waiting for? I don't see why we're here, I'm hungry. What d'y say we get some fish and chips?" Several others chimed in, eager to do something.

"Come on, Mick, we need some action!"

The gang restlessly regrouped around Mick as he spied the approaching shape of a body he recognised. A lanky, spotty wimp, Becky's bodyguard brother drew nearer to the bench.

"What's he doing here?" one of them demanded.

Mick stepped forward as the youth made his way over through the threatening group.

"You've no business coming here, I made the arrangement with Becky, is she going to be late or something?" Mick searched her brother's face for a sign.

He could hear the whispers behind him,

"It's a date, he really wants this bird." The snickers and nudging didn't go unnoticed. Harry gathered up his wits, working out exactly what he would say to get what he wanted out of Mick.

"I made the date, Becky doesn't know anything about it, that's why I'm here."

"Piss off, you slimy nerd. What would a homo like you know about real dates? Becky made the date, I've seen her look at me."

More sniggers from the gang, he could see from the corner of his eye, that Tommo was assessing the scene, getting ready!

Harry summoned up his remaining nerves, ignoring the jibes about him.

"Let me explain. Fuck off," he swung round to confront the lemmings encroaching around his back.

Falteringly, he stuttered out his proposition, that he would pay Mick to see off the bullies bothering Becky. Pandering to Mick's ego, he argued that no one would chance anymore rumours if Mick let them know she was under his protection.

"Becky should have come, she should ask me herself," Mick stubbornly continued.

"Look she doesn't want a boyfriend," Harry lamely went on, "she's just trying to catch up with school work, it isn't that there's someone else. Just leave her alone," he faded off, avoiding the obvious. The excitement that had been building inside Mick crashed down. He had believed that Becky had seen through his image, had viewed him with at least some interest or attraction. He would have looked after her, treated her well, shown that he wasn't a lout like those around him. Mick was desolate now, all his dreams were taken away, washed down the drain as worthless. She was like all the other girls, a tease. Just another person laughing behind his back. Mick had no sense of humour, it had never developed. There were only two kinds, either you laughed at someone else or you were the subject of their laughter. He couldn't tolerate the latter, respect for him was like food and water, it was paramount.

"She's too good for you, she won't even talk to you!" Tommo spat out the words taunting him further. "You're only fit to talk to her faggot brother."

Hoots and loud guffaws rang from around Tommo and, as if in unison, thunder claps boomed through the air above them. The atmosphere was charged with electricity and tension. Further comments between the pack provoked louder peals of laughter and coarse signs at Mick's expense. The dark mist of his childhood descended in his head. Large bodies holding him down pummelling him, in fits of laughter at his puny naked body. Words knifing through his tears, cutting out any sense of worth or value.

"You're nothing runt, even Mum didn't want you. You killed her"

The scene repeated and expanded over the early years until it was the norm for this runt of the litter. No respect could be earned whatever the action or words he tried to learn to stop the persistent abuse. It was a game, hilarious to his brothers, whilst Mick was invisible, deserving of this practice. Rolls of thunder quickened in intervals interspersed with steaks of lightning across the charcoal grey sky. The fuse within Mick had been detonated in tandem with the elemental atmospheric pressure.

In seconds, he hurled himself towards an unsuspecting Harry, charging aside the pack of animals now chanting and snarling at Mick and Harry alike. They had become fused as a pair to be exploited and destroyed by the herd mentality. Harry's thin stringy body was no match for the wild onslaught and he hit the floor as the blows rained down on him while huge splashes of water began to fall. They wrestled and rolled over, he fought with all his strength to counter the assault. Around them the increasing volume of voices, urging them on, reached a crescendo.

Mick's compulsion to halt the ridicule crushed any sense in him, he felt for the knife and pulled it out!

The charges of energy radiated from the sprawling angry humans on the ground. Sounds and smells of fear mixed with tastes of sweat and toil.

Underneath the spread of branches, the lightning struck tree and human alike. Both had to withstand its energy and force, bowing to its undeniable power, whilst the battle to win and prove superiority from one human over another continued. The force of their efforts filled the thunderous atmosphere, recharging their batteries.

Decades before, a tree had witnessed a comparable struggle as workers fought for their rights over their employers. Deprivation for their families, despite working every hour possible, had forced them to fight for fairness. Unable to meet in public, an oath of secrecy hid their efforts. No freedom of expression was afforded them as in modern times. The seed of banding together in mutual agreement led to the first trade unions to seek for justice.

The situation, so alike in content, misused the freedom that was now given. The commonality of the two occasions displayed the recurrence of bullies in every generation, each seeking power and status. It remained an indictment to human frailty.

Chapter 16

9.00 p.m.

Dave skulked around the obscured area of the park where the water fountain was sited. His tongue and throat relieved from the drink he had gulped down. The ever growing storm hung above with distant thunder rolls approaching by the minute. It seemed hard to breathe and his clothes and the atmosphere weighed him down and were an unnecessary nuisance. Dave's senses were in overdrive, the smell and taste drew him into the memories of the conflict in Afghanistan He could almost touch the fear revisited in the gloom.

Steaks of silver flew across the sky high above then struck the ground like flashes of gun fire. The explosions of munitions multiplied, swelling in sound as the thunder intensified. The lightning, like paint running across a canvas, illuminated the dusty particles on the earth. It had been so similar in that foreign land. Clouds of dust had obliterated clear vision to search out the enemy. There was no escape from the crashes and bangs. When there was a respite they waited for the next onslaught. Dave couldn't see, the murkiness descended lower, persuading him to rest until his head cleared. Under the tree canopy, Dave could just make out a collection of figures clad in dark clothes and camouflage jackets. Jeers and shouts echoed towards his hiding place and he watched the circle of bodies closing into the centre of the group. The threats were palpable. Time became suspended. In grotesque slow motion he viewed the pantomime as utter weariness of the day overtook him. In his muddled brain, he believed he had been here before.

The figures were moving quickly now, in and out, in a macabre dance. Legs flailing out, bodies bent over with stabbing fists to a huddled form on the ground. A central figure towered over the vulnerable bundle beneath him, as a flash of metal reflected across the park. Thunder boomed as more lightning flashed and struck across the scene. Huge drops of water rained down vertical to the earth beneath. The heavy oppressive rain drops blinded any view, thrashing to the ground, crashing and bending the tree's branches to its will. The frenzy of the onslaught increased the tension, matched by the response of the humans under its spell.

"Man down," Dave clearly heard those traumatic words, though no syllables leapt from lips, only guttural animal noises.

He sprang from his undercover hiding place and charged across the space, intent on one thing, saving Sean his buddy. As the mad man approached, the circle opened up, baffled as the grubby form flew towards them. They had no time to think where he'd come from, they could only respond with blind panic. Mick, kicking and stomping at the prone body, hate of fifteen years welling up inside, was in a dark world of his own. He heard nothing, saw nothing, but controlled by his gut bile, a solid nugget burning and scorching his insides.

A voice in his head insisted that he listened.

'How stupid did he look to his mates?'

'How can this wimpy turd defy him?'

Respect was missing, Harry wasn't taking him seriously. Adrenalin raced through his body and he kicked harder!

Dave landed on Mick with a thud. His army training kicked in instinctively. Mindless of any safety to himself, his body flattened the demented attacker who was towering over the inert human. He touched a sticky substance under them as they rolled and struggled with the knife in Mick's hand. Past demons of Dave's life unleashed, he soon became the superior warrior. Mick was no match for him. Tumbling over and over in the dirt they strained in combat, unaware that the circle of onlookers had run off, flying in all directions from this unexpected onslaught. Mick glanced around and realised that he had to retreat and escape from this maniac. He was on his own now. Mustering his remaining strength, he kneed Dave in the groin and lurched out of his grip. Reeling forwards, he spurted away from the spot, gathering up the remnants of any energy and sprinted away from the scene.

As Dave recovered from his buckled state of pain, the figure beside him came into focus. The twisted form of arms and legs lay quiet and still, a pool of blood seeping out was growing larger. A certainty grew that this time he'd succeeded, the enemy had been routed and defeated. They had run away like the cowards they were.

He knew it wasn't Sean in his heart, but it was the next best thing.

Redeeming himself, the quiet voice was stilled.

★★★★★★★★★★★★

A figure knelt beside him, he could hear words whispered into a phone. Gentle hands helped him sit up and gradually the mist burned off. The soggy ground underneath him was exchanged for the bench, the rain had stopped as the sky discharged its load. The thunder and lightning had moved on to threaten somewhere else and fresh air gave a welcome lift to plants and creatures alike.

Dave looked up into the eyes of Bob, an older Bob, but definitely the same familiar face of his school mate. The anger inside that he'd once felt for this man couldn't be summoned, he felt secure and relief trickled through him. Bob had made his way with the kids through the park to find Sophie and walk her home from Granddad Keith's house. He had so much to tell her now the meeting was over. An extra few minutes together as a family would give a chance for the kids to talk to their mum before their bedtime. The commotion near the sycamore tree had suddenly demanded his attention. He quickly realised that it was more than idle youths messing around and raced to help.

A young man on the ground and youths disappearing in every direction, he nearly fell over a second human bundle on the earth. The tramp's eyes were shut, blood covered his hands and clothes. Bob peered again at the stubbly beard and greasy hair slowly recognising the features. The revelation was unbelievable, it was hard to grasp the truth. Dave his old school mate was here! How could he forget that face? Pleased that his friend's eyes wouldn't meet his yet, Bob prepared for the scorn, hurt, or anger that he remembered on their last meeting.

Bob felt the second body near him, it was wet and cold with no response to his touch. People seemed to appear from out of nowhere. Across the park a woman ran towards him, it was Sophie still wearing her nurse's uniform. Their eyes met briefly as she knelt beside the half-dead youth. She worked on him with the skill and confidence of her training until the paramedics arrived and took over. Sophie now turned her attention to the bench where Dave was now slumped, as Bob hovered in the background. The man didn't seem to have any obvious major injuries though he was covered in blood. It was difficult to recognise bruises through the dirt on his skin. Eventually, it dawned on Sophie that the face before her answered her nightmares. She couldn't accept it was Dave, the shock at the state of him touched her deeply. Where was the youth she had once loved?

The police, having arrived were busy questioning the identity of the lifeless boy from the paramedics. The urgency of his condition prompted the need to call off further words as the ambulance made ready to drive off. Onlookers were gathering as they sped away, other details would have to be taken, they looked around assessing the crime scene.

Dave attempted to focus on himself and was steadily recovering from his exertions. He became conscious of a small girl at the side of her mother. As he glanced upwards, a boy peered over the shoulders of the woman. A face he knew. Puzzlingly, the features of the woman were familiar too. His sluggish thoughts were bewildered by their faces. In tortoise like rapidity his mind cleared. He stared at the eyes, nose and lips of his late father. Silence stretched tenuously between the three adults as Dave identified the faces of Sophie and Bob. A smile began to melt between Sophie's eyes and lips as she uttered the words he'd longed for,

"Dave, are you alright? How do you feel, is anything hurting?"

He turned from her, brushing aside her questions and stared at the boy searching every inch of his face.

"Yes, Dave, we've been looking for you for so long. This is your son." Sophie stuttered. Bob, attempting to clarify the confusion that hung in the air, hugged his friend, grinning from ear to ear. He whispered softly for only them to hear.

"Mate, Sophie's right. This is Peter, we share your son with you."

Everything happened at once, a police officer pushed through the trio and stood accusingly over Dave. Question after question poured out of his lips, notebook at the ready as he scribbled away. He was eager to judge an itinerant, history told him they caused trouble and extra work. Explanations were offered by witnesses and sought from householders assembled at the fringes. The park developed into chaos. It seemed ages before it was accepted that Dave needed to be checked at hospital, despite Bob's protest at the treatment of him and the time that had elapsed. A statement would have to wait until he was cleared by the doctors.

Bob and Sophie took over, they had rehearsed the meeting with Dave for many years. There was no way they would allow him to vanish again from their lives. Anticipating some resistance, they finally persuaded him to join Bob who would take him to a nearby hospital. It seemed reasonable to Sophie that she took the children home and calm them down after all the excitement. She would need to summon all her wisdom in the days to come to explain Dave's appearance to her son. There was such a lot to find out and accept for the three of them, so much to catch up on before she could hope to smooth the path for Peter and his newly found father. It was what the family had prayed for, but the obstacles in the future were inconceivable.

Dave settled in the passenger seat alongside Bob, pleased to accept help. He was hoping for relief from the aching ribs, cuts and bruises. Fear, sadness, joy and courage mulled around in his head. Overriding these emotions, one surfaced clearly from the others. A calming stillness settled, for the first time in many years in his heart.

Tomorrow would be a better day, he knew it in every fibre of his body!

The area was taped off around the tree, a crime scene to be studied tomorrow. The park now deserted and locked from any intruder was left for the natural inhabitants, the creatures. Rest and sleep for most, except for the nocturnal fraternity.

Cancellation of the fate of the tree, or a postponement? It stood silent awaiting a verdict.

The End

Acknowledgements

I have so many people to thank for their support and encouragement as I tackled my first novel. Joining a writing group recently helped to motivate and drive me onwards and I am grateful for their words of inspiration.

Particular appreciation must go to a circle of friends who patiently read and discussed my work in the early stages.

Thank you Bruce, Hazel, Maureen, Sue and Sylvia for your interest and enthusiasm. To Rachel and Jean who copy edited and proof read Silent Links, thank you for your helpful suggestions.

Finally special thanks go to my sons and grand children who spurred me on and for their reassurances. I am indebted to my husband for his patient constant support and practical help.